MISTER ORANGE

Jacket and interior art by Jenni Desmond

N ederlands
letterenfonds
dutch foundation
for literature

Enchanted Lion Books gratefully acknowledges the support of
the Dutch Foundation for Literature for the translation of this book.

Enchanted Lion Books would also like to thank Lawrence Kim,
Mercedes Pritchett, and Theo Zimmerman for their devotion and insight.

www.enchantedlion.com

First American edition published in 2012 by Enchanted Lion Books,
20 Jay Street, Studio M-18, Brooklyn, NY 11201
Text Copyright © 2011 by Truus Matti
Translation Copyright © 2012 by Laura Watkinson
Illustration Copyright © 2012 by Enchanted Lion Books
Originally published in 2011 in Dutch as *Mister Orange*
by Uitgeverij Leopold bv, Amsterdam
All rights reserved under International and
Pan-American Copyright conventions
A CIP record is on file with the Library of Congress

Printed in the United States of America
by Lake Book Manufacturing, Inc., Illinois

Mister Orange

Truus Matti

Translated from the Dutch by Laura Watkinson

ENCHANTED LION BOOKS
NEW YORK

NEW YORK
MARCH 1945

Linus is flying. He skims over puddles, glides over curbs, zigzags between people, dodges to avoid pedestrians. He is unstoppable. He has wings, and the faster he moves, the easier it feels. *Must be my shoes*, Linus thinks. They fit perfectly. Not too big now, nor too small, today it feels as if they were made just for him.

It's busy on Park Avenue. A woman shouts after him, "Young man! Watch where you're going!" But her voice sounds more amused than angry. How could anyone be angry on a day like this? The sun has finally realized that spring is here. Linus is running north, with the sun at his back lighting up the faces of the people walking toward him. The rain of the past few days lingers only in the puddles, which sparkle as they reflect the sunshine. Linus wants to go down to the water, to watch the sun glinting off the ripples of the East River.

He makes a right turn. In the side streets, the sun's golden light shines through wherever it finds space between the buildings. Linus continues to run, crossing Lexington and then Third. He is already past Second when he finally has to stop to catch his breath. He stands with his hands on his knees, panting in the middle of the sidewalk. Someone bumps into him and a boy yells something he doesn't catch. Linus stands up straight to look at the boy, but something else attracts his attention. Something in a large display window. Linus walks over to take a look. There are a few paintings on display, and a poster in one corner announcing something in big black letters. But what caught his eye was the photograph beside the poster. A familiar face looks out at him from behind a pair of dark-framed glasses, as though it's perfectly natural for him to be there. The smile twitching at one corner of the mouth is easy to miss unless you look very closely. Linus can't help smiling back. Seeing that face feels so... normal, as though it was only yesterday that it had looked out at him from around the door. *Linus! Come in...*

There is an address on the poster: 11 West 53rd Street.

The East River can wait. Linus turns around. First he has to walk all the way over to Fifth Avenue, before heading south. But with his perfect shoes and the sun on his face, he'll be there in no time.

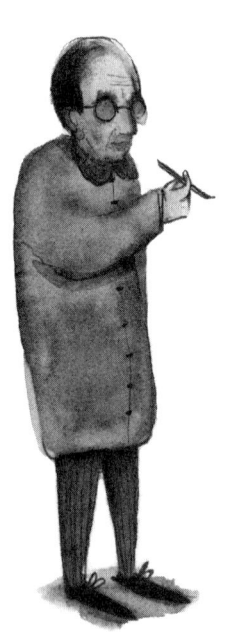
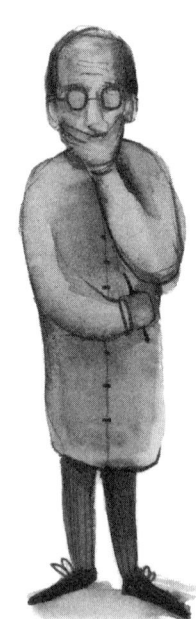

NEW YORK
SEPTEMBER 1943

1

WHEN ALBIE WENT OFF to war, everyone at home got new shoes. Not new-new, like Albie's gleaming army boots, which smelled of fresh leather and felt really stiff, but the kind of new that Linus's family was used to, with one person's old shoes becoming new shoes for the next one in line.

As far as Linus was concerned, it was about time he had new shoes. He'd gotten into the habit of walking on the outside of his feet so his shoes wouldn't pinch his toes with every step. He told himself that no one had noticed, but Rosie Donnelly soon set him straight. "Hey, Linus Muller!" she yelled. "Someone step on your toes? Or do you just have to go potty?"

"Aw, ignore her," said Liam when he saw Linus's red face. That was easy enough for Liam to say. He'd grown up with his big sister's sharp tongue, and it took a lot for her to upset him now.

"Is that you, Linus?" his mother called downstairs as he opened the door. It was Saturday afternoon and the store was busy. His father was behind the counter, weighing tomatoes for a customer. *Hurry up!* he signaled to Linus with his eyes. The language they used in the store was all about signs and glances. *Linus, you know your mother doesn't like to be kept waiting!* She'd probably been shouting the same question down the stairs for the past half hour, every time a new customer came in.

Yes, yes, I'm on my way! Linus waved to his father and walked through the store. Simon was out back in the storeroom stacking crates. Linus climbed upstairs, lugging his heavy shopping bag. Four pairs of boys' shoes were arranged at the top, in order of size, from small to large.

"What took you so long?" His mother came out of the kitchen carrying a burlap sack. "I told you to come straight home after doing the shopping. You're keeping Albie waiting, and the shoe repairman, too. How's he supposed to mend all of these shoes in one afternoon if he gets them late?"

"Everywhere was so busy." Linus kicked off his shoes and placed them in his mother's outstretched hand. Then he gently pinched his toes and wiggled them until he could feel them again.

"Simon's been back for ages and he had farther to go." Luckily his mother was too busy inspecting his shoes to keep asking questions. Linus had been to visit Liam on the way home and they'd gone to Fifth Avenue to see if there was any sign of the military parade yet. All of the side streets had been closed off and a few newspaper photographers were wandering around, but it was going to be a while before the soldiers got there.

Linus had leaned over the barrier with Liam, the shopping bag on the ground between his feet. Without any automobiles around, the avenue looked even wider than usual. He imagined the thousands of soldiers who would be marching along there soon, row upon row of them, all the way to Washington Square

Park. The soldiers who would be leaving on enormous ships that very night to go to Europe and join the fight against Hitler.

But before that, this very afternoon, the entire city of New York would turn out to cheer them on their way. All of New York, that is, except for Linus, who had to stay at home because his shoes were being mended.

He had moaned and begged all week for his mother to send the shoes to be repaired a week later, but she wouldn't budge. "I don't care for all these parades," she had said. His mother didn't like war. "And we all need to look our best when we take Albie to the train on Sunday."

His mother completed her inspection and dropped the last pair of shoes into the sack.

"Albie?" She held out the bag. "New soles and heels, check the stitching, and new laces."

"Albert," Albie corrected her. Now that he was eighteen and joining the army, he wanted to be called by his proper name, but everyone kept forgetting.

"O'Leary's on 75th Street. He's waiting for them, so hurry up."

Albie took the sack without saying a word. He'd been wearing his uniform for a few days, and it was clear that he thought an errand like this was beneath a real soldier. But he had to do it. He was the only one of the boys who still had a pair of shoes.

Linus watched longingly as Albie left the house. The whole city was full of heroes, but Linus was stuck at home in his socks.

The floor of the storeroom felt cold on Linus's feet, even though he was wearing three pairs of socks. He had already polished a mountain of apples, which should keep his father going for a week. Whenever the bell rang, he took a step back and looked to see who had come in. If Albie was quick, Linus might still catch the end of the parade.

But when Liam dropped by at four-thirty to see if Linus could come out yet, there was still no sign of Albie. Liam said he'd seen him going into Werther's earlier that afternoon. Werther's sold magazines and tobacco, and it was also the place where everyone went to hear the latest news about the neighborhood and about the war. Albie must have gone there to show off his uniform. *Just so long as he doesn't forget the shoes*, Linus thought as he listened to his friend. Liam's cheeks flushed as he told Linus about the rows of soldiers carrying real guns and marching so crisply it gave you goose bumps. He said he'd been standing so close that he'd felt the beating of the drums in his chest.

When Liam finished telling his story, he grew antsy. Linus could see how anxious he was to get back to the parade. If Albie didn't return soon, Liam would go on his own. "Well, is he coming?" Liam kept asking. "It's going to be dark soon…"

By the time Albie finally got home, Liam was long gone.

"Can I still go out, just for a little while?" begged Linus. "I promised Liam. Just as far as Fifth for a quick look? I'll come straight back."

"It's your brother's last evening at home," his mother said. She picked up Sissie from the baby chair. "And that means everyone's staying in. Including Albie." She turned to look at Albie, who was already standing at the top of the stairs, hoping to slip out unnoticed—as if he hadn't already showed off his uniform to the whole city!

"Albert," Albie muttered. His mother didn't answer, but handed Sissie to him and started emptying the sack of shoes.

Albie might be leaving with the army tomorrow, but today his mother was still in charge. Not even a new uniform and a pair of shiny boots were going to change that.

2

THE NEW SHOES SMELLED of glue and polish. Linus had stuffed the toes with newspaper and tied the laces as tightly as possible, but it still felt as though his feet were swimming around. On top of that, the tips of the shoes curved upward. Simon's funny upturned toes had pushed them up, day after day, and now Linus's toes had the job of pushing them back down. He could already imagine Rosie laughing at him. *Look at Linus! His ears stick out and now he's got stuck-up toes to match!*

It was the last Sunday in September. The streets were busy, so the family walked in a neat line, one behind the other in order of size, from big to small, as they did for every important occasion. Their father was at the front, with Albie just behind, his kitbag over his shoulder. In his new army cap, Albie's head was just a little higher than their father's.

It was a long way to Grand Central Station, and their father seemed to be walking faster and faster. Max, who was walking behind Linus, kept tripping over his own feet and grabbing Linus by the waist.

Max's new shoes were Linus's old ones, and all Sunday morning he had complained that they were much too big. He had demanded his own shoes back, but he couldn't have them because they now belonged to Willy.

"You're going too fast for the little ones, Bertie!" their mother called over their heads to the front of the line. She was bringing up the rear with Sissie in her arms and pushing Willy along in front of her. The gap between Willy and Max was growing larger and larger. When Willy started crying, their father finally stopped and picked him up. With Willy on his shoulders, their father towered above everyone again, even Albie.

Albie wasn't going straight onto the boat to Europe. He had to go to a training camp first, with other soldiers like him who had never fought in a war. Linus thought it was a real shame that Albie hadn't marched in the parade and would be leaving on the train just like any normal traveler.

But when they entered the enormous space of Grand Central Station, he suddenly felt very serious and solemn, as if they were stepping into a cathedral. Rays of sunlight slanted in through the windows high above. Voices and footsteps echoed all around, and he could hear snatches of music in the distance. The family merged with the rest of the crowd, drawing closer together as they made their way through the magnificent building.

The platform was green with army uniforms. The atmosphere was nervous, agitated, excited. Lots of people were shouting and laughing, all at the same time. At the end of the platform an army band played marching music.

Their father lined them all up neatly again, and then they stood there, not quite knowing what to say or do. The whole neighborhood had come to Albie's farewell party the night before. There had been so many good wishes that now it seemed there was nothing left to say.

"Well, my boy." Their father held out his hand to Albie. "This is it. Remember to dodge those bullets." It was a joke that their neighbor had made yesterday. Albie nodded a little sheepishly, hugged his father, and then worked his way down the line as quickly as he could. Their mother, still holding Sis, wrapped her free arm around his neck. Sis grabbed at Albie's hair with her sticky little fists, and when he finally released himself, she snatched at his cap and knocked it off with a shriek of delight. Albie dived into the crowd and surfaced a short distance away, laughing and waving his cap above his head. He was swept away from them in the stream of soldiers, toward the waiting train and up the steps, where he disappeared inside. A little later, he stuck his head out of a window, but before he could say anything someone pulled him away, and a stranger's head appeared in his place.

The music stopped. Linus thought someone might make a speech—the mayor, or maybe a general. But instead, one by one, all of the train doors slammed shut. A whistle blew, the wheels began to grind, and slowly the train started to move. People ran alongside the train, shouting and waving. Linus had to keep an eye on Willy, who was almost knocked over in the commotion. When he looked up again, the train was chugging into the distance, and his big brother was nowhere to be seen.

"Albie!" Linus cried, but his voice was lost in the noise. He felt a heavy lump sink to the pit of his stomach. The feeling spread to his arms and legs. All at once he realized how many things he'd forgotten to say, and now it was too late.

"Albert," their mother said with a sigh. It seemed as if she had to correct Linus now that Albie wasn't there to do it himself.

They watched the train until the tunnel swallowed it up.

Their father coughed a few times. Then he made little circles in the air with his forefinger, and they all turned around. In single file, like their own little army, they marched down the platform and through the enormous station to the exit. They were arranged from small to big this time, their mother at the front with Sis, who was making a sound that was somewhere between crying and humming. Max was in front of Linus now and whenever he tripped he stepped on Willy's heels, causing Willy to turn around and glare at him. "Hey!" Willy yelped over and over, his voice rising higher and higher, until their father finally picked him up and lifted him back onto his shoulders. Linus wasn't the only one who had to get used to wearing someone else's shoes.

At home, the decorations from the farewell party hung drearily in the silent living room. Their mother took off her coat and filled the emptiness with instructions for everyone. She gave Sis to Max and told him to watch her and Willy. Simon's job was to take down the decorations, and no matter how much the little ones protested she remained firm. "War is not a cause for celebration," she said as she handed Linus a pile of sheets and pushed him toward Albie and Simon's bedroom. It was a tiny room with only a bunk bed and a closet. Linus stared at the bottom bunk, which Albie had stripped just that morning. The bare pillow rested on top of a blanket at the foot of the bed. The painful lump in Linus's stomach was still there. It felt strange to be making Albie's bed, the bed that Albie had slept in only last night, the bed that was now going to be his. From now on, he wouldn't be sleeping in the little ones' room anymore.

"It sags a bit, but it's cozy. You'll get a good night's sleep in it," Albie had said to him that morning, patting the space beside him on the unmade bed.

"Will you keep an eye on my *Action Comics?*" he had asked as Linus sat down next to him. "I'll leave them under the bed, but make sure the little ones don't get their hands on them. If they do, they'll get them all stained and sticky, and they'll tear the pictures out, too."

Linus nodded gravely.

"No point asking Simon." Albie had nodded at the bunk above. Linus knew exactly what Albie meant. Simon thought comics were childish. Albie was more than three years older than Simon, but he loved comics, just like Linus. *That's probably because Albie's too grown-up to think things are childish*, thought Linus.

"And I want you to buy the new one every month." Linus had stared in amazement as Albie produced two dollar bills. "Don't forget."

"Of course not!" Linus carefully tucked the two bills into his pocket. He was proud to have been entrusted with Albie's comics collection. Albie and Linus's favorite strips were the ones about Superman. Since America had joined the war, they mostly had been about Superman helping to fight the Nazis.

Linus tucked in the blanket and sat down on his new bed. Then he leaned over the edge and looked under it. There they were, in two neat piles, with all the issues in the right order, starting with the very first one from 1938.

On top of one of the piles, Albie had stacked his own sketchbooks, which were just old notebooks that he sometimes took from the mailroom at the newspaper where he worked. No one needed the notebooks anymore, even though they were often less than half full. Albie had asked for them a few times and after that everybody at the paper had kept them for him. They all knew Albie liked to draw. Linus reached out and carefully took a notebook from the top of the pile. Albie had filled the empty pages with pencil sketches of his own superhero, one he'd invented himself: Mister Superspeed. "Superman could do with a little help now that there's a war on," Albie had joked. Albie wanted to be a comics artist when the war was over, and Linus thought he was getting better and better at drawing. In the first notebook, Mister Superspeed had arms that were far too long, or maybe it was his head that was too small. And whenever he tried to run, his legs got all tangled up. Linus could see that Albie had used his eraser a lot and penciled over the old lines.

By the second notebook, Mister Superspeed was already looking a lot better. He stood there grinning, with his legs apart and his clenched fists on his hips, sometimes with his helmet under one arm. From his sleek costume, you could see that he came from the future. Powered by the clouds of steam that shot out of the soles of his boots, he soared confidently into the sky and captured enemy soldiers in his vise-like grip. Linus slowly turned the pages. The more he saw, the more Mister Superspeed looked as though he really might be able to help. Linus stopped at a drawing near the back of the book. It was a really great one. Mister Superspeed was straddling the nose of an airplane that had a large swastika, the symbol of the Nazis, on its side. Since the Nazis were America's enemy, they were Mister Superspeed's enemy too. Mister Superspeed was holding the pilot firmly by his collar. The pilot was clearly in big trouble.

Almost perfect, thought Linus. He traced the pencil lines with his finger and tried to work out what was missing.

He held the notebook at an angle. Seen from the side, Mister Superspeed looked a bit like Albie. It was his expression. He had the same determined look that Albie had so often in his eyes.

"*Don't you worry. I'll keep an eye on your brother.*" *Mister Superspeed looks at Linus out of the corner of his eye without loosening his grip on the pilot.*

"*Promise?*" *Linus asks.*

"*It'll be our secret.*" *Mister Superspeed raises his forefinger to his lips and winks at Linus.* "*This guy,*" *he says, giving the pilot a shake,* "*certainly isn't going to be talking to anyone.*" *The pilot groans. He's a real coward—you can tell just by looking at him. Black smoke billows from the plane and the engine is making strange noises. The pilot screams and cries for mercy. The plane takes a nosedive.*

"*Our secret!*" *Linus has to shout to make himself heard above the noise.*

"What's that about secrets?" Simon flung the door open with a bang. "If you're going to act like a baby, maybe you better go back to the little ones." He grabbed a sweater from the closet and pulled it on. As he passed Linus, Simon glanced down at the notebook on his knees.

"Mister Superspeed. I should have known. How super childish." The door slammed shut behind him.

Linus paid no attention. With a contented sigh, he lay back with his arms beneath his head and the notebook on his chest. The awful feeling in his stomach had almost disappeared.

3

"Why don't smells have names?"

Linus was sitting on the counter, playing with an orange that he'd taken from the crate beside him. The more he threw it into the air, the stronger its smell became. It was late afternoon. The window blind was halfway down, so Linus could see only the middle sections of the people going by. He watched the headless, legless bodies making their way past the store.

He had already helped his father prepare the orders that he was going to deliver tomorrow after school for the very first time. It wasn't just shoes that had been handed down when Albie left. Jobs had been reassigned, too. Linus was taking over Simon's delivery route, and Simon had taken over Albie's job in the mailroom at the newspaper. Now that Linus was one of the big ones, Max was officially the biggest of the little ones, so he would have to take care of Willy and Sis after school.

Linus's father didn't answer. He was looking through the pile of order forms with a frown on his face. His father never said much. The few words he had were generally reserved for his customers, with hardly any left for home.

"But it's strange, isn't it?" Linus wrapped his fingers around the orange and thoughtfully breathed in its scent. "There are words for colors, but not for smells. The way this orange smells, for instance." Linus held it up. "There's just no word for that."

"Well, I suppose you'd call it... fruity." His father had started making a list for the next day. Every morning, he got up at the crack of dawn and went downtown to the big wholesale market to buy fruit and vegetables.

"But that's just one word for everything!" Linus insisted. "Every fruit has its own smell, doesn't it? What I mean is that there should be a special word for every smell."

"You ask more questions than is good for a man." His father sighed. "Why don't you just go upstairs and look after the little ones?" he added automatically. Linus hated it when his father said that. It was his usual response when he didn't want to answer questions. But this time Linus could feel himself starting to grin.

"The little ones? That's Max's job now." Linus really enjoyed saying that for the first time.

His father looked up from his list, irritated, and put his pencil behind one ear. Linus couldn't help laughing. He drummed on the counter with both hands.

"Stop making all that noise!" His father shook his head, but he couldn't help smiling, which made Linus laugh even more. It felt good to make noise, to break the silence that had hung in the house all afternoon.

Linus heard someone running down the stairs. Then Simon dashed through the store, on his way out.

"Did you take this order yesterday, Simon?" His father held up an order form. "It's for 59th Street. You know how important it is to write the name of the customer clearly, don't you?"

Simon looked at the piece of paper and shrugged. "It was a new customer. He had some kind of funny accent. I got him to repeat his name three times, but I still couldn't get what he was saying. So I asked him to write it himself."

His father raised his eyebrows. "Couldn't he find somewhere closer to home to buy his fruit and vegetables? This is more than ten blocks away." He looked down at the piece of paper again. "Are you sure he wants an entire crate of oranges?"

Simon nodded. "He wants to squeeze them for juice." Then he unlocked the door and headed out into the street without saying goodbye.

"That's all the oranges we've got," his father grumbled. He took the pencil from behind his ear and added something to the list.

"Don't forget to ask our new customer for his real name tomorrow." His father put the order form on the pile. Linus took a look. "Every other Monday. Deliver after half past four," it said in Simon's scrawl. He'd underlined the word "after" twice.

"And make him the last delivery on your route," his father added. "Then you can stop off at the store to pick up the crate so you won't have to drag it around with you. More than ten blocks…" He gave Linus a searching look. "You sure you can manage by yourself tomorrow?"

Linus nodded. He knew the neighborhood well enough to find his own way around. With his eyes closed, if necessary. What could possibly go wrong?

4

LINUS'S SHOES WERE TAKING the exact same route as before, only with his feet inside them now instead of Simon's. *Nothing has changed for my shoes*, thought Linus, as he pulled the cart along the sidewalk behind him. The cart was loaded high and steering it took some getting used to. He really had to pay attention. Occasionally his feet forgot they were in new shoes, and he almost stumbled over a curb or a loose paving stone.

O'Reilly's Restaurant was at the top of his list. A large bag of onions and a box of tomatoes. He got there in just a couple of minutes. He was about to carry the onions inside, but the girl who came to the door took the sack from him, put it on top of the tomato box, and picked up the whole thing. Then she smiled at him and closed the door with her foot.

So far, everything seemed to be going smoothly. There were two more addresses nearby. The first was Castelli's and he knew where that was. It was an Italian restaurant four blocks away. "Deliver before four," it said on the back of the order form. According to the list, he had to go to Mrs. De Winter's after that. For just a pound of plums and a bag of grapes. But that address was only two blocks from the corner where he was standing. If he went there first, he wouldn't have to go back all that way for such a small order. And if he hurried, he'd have no trouble getting to Castelli's in time. Then he'd have done all of his addresses to the north by four o'clock, and he'd be back at the store in record time to pick up the crate of oranges for 59th Street. His father would be amazed.

Linus had to wait for a while before the door finally opened. Mrs. De Winter was the same height as Linus. She was shaking with old age and her cheeks were wrinkled.

"Yes?" she said, peering at him suspiciously.

"Your order, ma'am." Linus held up the bags. Plums on the left, grapes on the right.

"It was always another boy. Another boy used to come." The woman shifted her gaze from Linus to the bags of fruit. "What happened to the other boy?"

"I'm the new delivery boy." Linus smiled and waved the bags to prove it, but she didn't smile back.

"Well, well, isn't that nice? They change everything and nobody tells me a thing. How am I supposed to know if it's true?" Her voice didn't sound at all shaky or wrinkly now. It sounded loud and clear. And pretty angry, too.

"I'm Linus Muller. Simon's brother." Linus lowered the bags of fruit.

"Simon? Simon? How should I know who that is? No one ever tells me anything," she grumbled.

"Simon. The boy who used to come." Linus held up the bags again. Finally she reached out a hand and took one of them. She opened the bag very slowly and stood there for a while, glowering at her plums. Linus hopped impatiently from one foot to the other.

"Come on, then." She slowly closed the bag again, turned around and beckoned to Linus to follow her. "You'll just have to give me a hand this time instead."

Linus hesitated. How long was this going to take? He didn't dare protest, so he threw the canvas over his cart and followed her down the narrow hallway, the bag of grapes still in his hand. It smelled musty inside her apartment. A huge set of antlers hung on the wall with coats dangling from it. He had to duck to get past. The old woman slowly shuffled ahead of him into the living room. It was packed with furniture and she had to squeeze her way through to the kitchen. "It's just me here," she said. "All on my own." Linus nodded politely, but he wondered why someone all on their own had so many chairs and tables. Maybe she had a lot of visitors.

She pointed at the garbage can in the kitchen. "I don't have anyone to do it for me," she said, as though that was Linus's fault. Linus gave her the grapes and picked up the garbage can. It was so heavy that he had to put it down to rest after just a couple of steps.

"Be careful, will you?" The woman was right behind him. "I don't want any mess in my house." Linus nodded and weaved his way back through the living room as carefully and quickly as he could. Finally he reached the hallway. He was a little out of breath. "Just leave it there. My neighbor can empty it for me later. And make sure you close the door behind you!" She put her hands on her hips and watched him leave.

Now Linus understood why her name had been at the bottom of the list. By the time he finally got back to his cart, the clock on Werther's Cigar Store said it was five to four. He was never going to make it! He hurried along the sidewalk, pulling the cart behind him. It was hard to run and to steer around all those feet at the same time. "Watch where you're going!" a woman with a baby carriage called after him. A dog ran barking around his cart and its leash got tangled up in one of the wheels. Linus felt hotter and hotter.

It was eight minutes past four when he reached Castelli's. A man in a white apron stood waiting for him on the sidewalk in front of the restaurant. There were big red stains over his belly.

"You're late. I've been standing here for ages." The man leaned over the cart. In all the hurry, some lemons had bounced out of the box on top. Linus felt himself blushing as he picked up the escaped lemons and put them back. The man lifted the bag of onions and the boxes of leeks and lemons off the cart and balanced everything on one arm.

"What about the plum tomatoes?" he said.

Linus bent down to pick up the last box on the cart.

"No, no." The man held up his free hand to stop Linus. "Not soup tomatoes. Plum tomatoes."

Linus felt his face becoming even hotter.

"Plum tomatoes are long, big. Soup tomatoes are small, round. These—these aren't my tomatoes!" The man's arm fell limply to his side.

Linus stared at the cart as if he could change the shape of the tomatoes just by looking at them hard enough.

"I think I must have gotten them mixed up with O'Reilly's tomatoes," he mumbled.

"O'Reilly? O'Reilly has my *pomodori*?" The man's dark eyes bored into Linus's. Lifting up the box of soup tomatoes in one hand, he thrust it into Linus's arms. Then he loaded the other things back onto the cart and stood in front of it, his fists on his hips. "Well? What are you still doing here? Go get them! Run!"

Now that it was after four, the streets were even busier than before. And they were only going to get busier as people left work and headed home. Linus hugged the box of tomatoes to his chest and puffed and panted his way through the stream of pedestrians. His shoes were rubbing against his heels. The box felt heavier and heavier. But he kept running, as fast as he could, maybe even faster.

"No need to wash them," Linus said, in an attempt at humor, when he got back to Castelli's exactly fourteen minutes later. Gasping for breath, he held up the box of plum tomatoes. "They already had them draining in the sink."

"Wise guy." The man wasn't exactly laughing, but he didn't look quite as angry as before. "It's your first day, so it's all right this time, but don't let it happen again." He picked up Linus's cart and lifted it back outside as though it weighed nothing. Then he slammed the door.

Linus leaned over the cart. All that racing around had made him feel sick. He took off his jacket and threw it onto the cart. He had somehow managed to cut his hand open on a fence as he was squeezing his way through the crowd around a subway entrance, and he was just starting to feel the pain now. His knees were shaking with exhaustion as he began the walk home, dragging the cart behind him.

CHAPTER 4

When Linus got back to the store at a quarter to five, he was relieved to see that his father had already headed upstairs. His mother looked after the store in the late afternoons so that their father could catch up on the sleep he missed by getting up so early for the market. He could sleep through anything. He wouldn't wake up even if Sissie and Willy used his bed as a trampoline.

His mother came out with the crate of oranges. "They have to go to 59th Street, number 15." She put the crate on the cart. "Do you want me to write it down for you or will you remember?"

"I'll remember." Linus wanted to get away as quickly as possible.

"Everything okay?" his mother asked as she headed back inside. Then she stopped and took a long, hard look at him. "You seem tired."

"Everything's great." Linus was not in the mood for questions. He knew that if she got him talking, he would somehow end up telling her all about his blunder.

"Simon will be back home soon. He can take that crate if you like."

Linus shook his head. Then he gave her a wave and took off again, this time in the opposite direction. He could feel a blister coming up on his heel. He almost missed his old shoes.

"Fourteen minutes. Not bad. Not bad at all for a beginner." Mister Superspeed hovers in the air just above the cart. Little steam clouds puff out of the heels of his boots.

"Couldn't you have come and helped me out a bit?" Linus asks.

"I was needed elsewhere." Mister Superspeed sits down on the edge of the cart. He takes off his helmet and rests it on his knees.

"What was so important?" Linus asks.

"More important than rescuing a box of tomatoes?" Mister Superspeed shrugs. "Oh, you know. The usual problems. A ship sinking in the Hudson, an airplane with engine trouble. Someone's big brother almost forgetting to dodge the bullets."

"Albie?" Linus cried out with a gasp. "He's okay, isn't he?" Then he looked around. Had he said that out loud?

Fortunately, everyone was in too much of a hurry to pay any attention to a boy who was talking to thin air. Mister Superspeed had vanished again.

5

59th Street was where Central Park began. At number 15, there was a big display window full of porcelain dolls and vases. The door to the upper stories was behind a gate. Linus pulled his cart through the gate and into an alcove, parking it where no one could see it from the street. He pressed the doorbell and waited for a while before the buzzer rang, allowing him to push the door open.

The entryway itself was dark, but light was coming down the stairs, along with the jangle of cheerful music. Linus started to climb, holding the crate of oranges tightly to his chest. His father had taught him that the closer you hold a load to your body, the easier it is to carry.

At the top of the stairs, he stopped. There were two doors on the landing. The music was coming from the door on the left, which was slightly ajar. Linus put down the crate and knocked. As he did so, his knock pushed the door open a little wider.

"Delivery!" he called inside. He could just see the beginning of a white hallway.

Someone turned the music down, and Linus heard a cough. Light, rapid footsteps came toward him.

"I believe the agreement was to deliver after half past four," said a soft voice. A head appeared around the door. Dark eyes stared out at Linus from a thin face. The man's black hair was combed straight back. With his large, sharp nose, he looked a little like a bird.

"It's almost five o'clock, sir." Linus took a step back.

"Is it that time already?" The man's eyes widened. Then, straightening his heavy glasses, he looked down at the crate by Linus's feet.

"Aha!" His face lit up. "Health!" The man threw the door open and strode past Linus onto the landing. "Put it down here, by the kitchen." He had a strong accent, as though he had not been living in America for very long. He rubbed his hands together as he watched Linus move the crate, and then he bent down to take a look. He was wearing a smock that hung loosely from his shoulders. It was so loose that it almost seemed like there was no body beneath it. The color was the same blue as the apron that Linus's father wore in the store, but it had a little round collar that reminded Linus of Sis's baby dresses. It didn't quite match the sharp face above.

"A crate full of health." The man looked much friendlier now. The oranges seemed to have cheered him up. "These are exactly what I need." He patted his chest, which made him start coughing. Linus nodded politely, turned around and started walking down the stairs.

"Wait a moment," said the soft voice.

Linus looked around, his foot hovering over the next step.

The man bent down and took an orange from the crate. He weighed it in his hand. Linus watched him anxiously. Was something wrong? He hadn't delivered the wrong box again, had he?

But when the man looked up, he was smiling. "For your trouble," he called out. "Catch!" He pulled back his arm and threw the orange in an elegant arc. Linus was surprised to see the orange coming toward him. The man had aimed just a little too high, but Linus wanted to show how good he was at catching. With a little jump, he plucked the orange from the air.

The jump was nothing. A little hop, nothing more. And that is why it was so annoying that he missed the step when he landed. He reached for the rail, but he had the orange in his hand, so he couldn't grab it. There was nothing he could do to keep himself from bumping ingloriously down the stairs from one step to the next. It was only when the stairs made a turn and he crashed into the wall that he came to a stop.

"Oh, oh, have you very much hurt yourself?" The man dashed down the stairs, his smock flapping. In spite of his surprise, Linus still noticed that the man's English sounded a little odd.

"It's these shoes," he groaned. He'd landed on his knee and it really was very painful. "They're new. My feet still aren't used to them." He rolled up the leg of his pants. It was a nasty scrape and he could see that his knee was going to bruise.

"No, no, it's all my fault." The man straightened his glasses again and studied Linus's knee. "That was so foolish of me. I know perfectly well that I can't throw. Can you stand up?" He helped Linus to his feet. So there was a strong pair of arms underneath that baggy smock after all. Linus also noticed that there was a sharp smell about the man, a little like paint.

"We're going to have to do something about that knee. You just come inside for a moment." The man helped Linus back up the stairs, pushed the door open and led him down a white hallway. The smell of paint was even stronger inside the apartment. There was a small room at the end of the hallway. Sunlight filtered through the white curtain in front of the window. The man pointed to a chair, and Linus limped over and sat down on the edge of the seat.

"I'll go and find a bandage for you. Glass of water?" Linus nodded. Only now did he realize how thirsty all that running had made him. While the man was away, he looked around the room.

All of the walls were painted white. White walls! No flowery wallpaper to be seen. No oak table with a dark-red cloth. Not even a rug on the wooden floor. And no mahogany sideboard up against the wall, like at his house. Like in the homes of everyone he knew. At Liam and Rosie's, at the neighbors. Everywhere else was so busy and packed and dark. Here it was so...

... light. And bright. And empty.

But not empty in a boring way. Not bare. More like...

... *calm*, thought Linus, leaning back in the chair. Everything except the floor was white. A small table with a stool, a low bookcase. Even the bedspread on the narrow bed was white.

But all across that whiteness, he could see colored squares and rectangles everywhere he looked. Grouped together or on their own, on the walls, on a cupboard door, on the mantelpiece. Little islands of color in an ocean of white. They gleamed in sunny yellow, they danced before his eyes in bright red and blue. It was as though they were so cheerful that they simply couldn't stay still.

Linus reached out and carefully touched a blue square on the wall beside him. It felt like cardboard and he could see that it was attached to the wall with tiny nails at the corners.

He leaned over to take a better look. There were little holes in the wall around the square as well as around the nails on the cardboard. The longer he looked, the more holes he spotted.

"So, how do you like it?" The man was standing in the doorway, a glass of water in one hand and a first-aid kit in the other. His head was cocked to the side.

Linus nodded. "I think the colors are beautiful," he said quietly. He paused for a moment, and then said, "It's like they're floating."

"That's because they're such strong colors," said the man. Linus could tell from the man's voice that his answer had pleased him. "These are the colors of the future. They're the only colors I use." He handed Linus the glass of water, pulled up the white stool and sat down beside him with the first-aid kit on his knees.

"I'm a painter," he said when he saw the puzzled look on Linus's face. He pointed at his smock. Linus could see splashes of white and colored paint. The same colors as were on the wall.

"I've just moved in here." He opened the first-aid kit and took out a small bottle. "And all of this," he said, waving the hand with the bottle in it around the room, "is supposed to make the place look more cheerful. It's still not quite how I'd like it to be." He bent over Linus's knee. "This is going to sting for a moment, I'm afraid."

Linus knew how iodine worked. If you watched, it just made it sting even more. So he looked away from his knee and focused on the colors. What had the man called them? Strong colors. No wonder Superman's costume was exactly those colors. Now he understood why. Blue, red and yellow. The colors of the future... He felt something cold dripping onto his knee and knew it would start to sting.

"The colors of the future?" he asked quickly.

The man nodded. "That's what I call them. In the future, everything's going to be different. This here," he said, waving the bottle around the room again, "is just the beginning. It's all about searching... trying things out..." He put away the bottle of iodine. His long, thin fingers nimbly pulled a white gauze dressing from its wrapper.

"It's a bit like a puzzle." The bandage was swinging in the air above Linus's knee. "A puzzle with lots and lots of different combinations. Do you understand?"

Linus hesitated. Now at least he understood why all those holes in the wall were there.

"Do you mean it's a sort of game?" he asked.

The man smiled. It was a small smile that lifted only one corner of his mouth very slightly. He carefully placed the dressing on Linus's wound. Linus didn't feel anything. When the man looked up, Linus could also see the smile in his eyes, even though they were behind those serious glasses.

"That's not a bad way of looking at it," he said slowly. He cut off two strips of plaster and fastened the dressing with careful precision.

"There you go." He closed the first-aid kit and put it on the table, nice and straight. Just like everything else on the table, Linus realized. The man's books and papers were all arranged in neat piles, as though someone had just tidied up. He thought about their own messy living room at home. He could almost hear his mother complaining that she might as well not bother straightening up because the boys would only make a mess of everything all over again. The thought of home made him jump. How long had he been gone?

"My cart!" He had completely forgotten that he had left it downstairs all that time. He had forgotten everything. Everything outside of the room…

"I have to go!" Linus stood up, the glass still in his hand. Could he just put it down on that neat table? He handed it to the man, then dashed down the hallway and out of the front door.

"Be careful now!" Linus heard the man call as he raced down the stairs.

The cart was still where he had left it. With a sigh of relief, Linus steered it back out through the gate and onto the sidewalk. He looked up at the front of the building. There was nothing special about it from the outside, nothing to suggest the strange white world within. *And yet*, thought Linus as he walked down the street, *it's as though everything around me looks just a little bit different.*

Then he remembered about the name. He had forgotten to ask the man what he was called.

6

"You look like you're limping," Linus's mother said that night as he stood up to go to bed. He was so tired that all he wanted to do was lie down.

"I fell this afternoon." His knee felt a bit stiff.

"In the street? Oh, Linus!" his mother exclaimed.

"No, on the stairs. At that orange man's place. It's not too bad, just a scrape." Linus waved his hand, hoping she'd stop asking questions.

"Let me take a look." His mother pushed him back down onto the chair.

"There's nothing to see." Linus rolled up the leg of his pants. "He put a bandage on it. Ow, don't touch!" he cried as his mother's curious fingers started to pull at one corner of the bandage. She moved her hand away.

"Well, it looks like he did a good job," she said.

Linus nodded. He thought about those precise hands. "He was really nice, too," he said. Then he paused. Should he tell her about the rest of it? About the white room and the strong colors? He decided to keep quiet.

His mother folded her arms and looked at him. "Is the

delivery round too much for you?"

"Of course not," said Linus. He stood up again. "I just need a little while to get used to it."

"It wasn't too far, was it? All that way with a crate of oranges?" Now his father had decided to join in.

"No, of course it wasn't." Did they think he was completely useless?

"Did you ask the man for his name?" his father asked. His pen hovered expectantly over his order book.

"No, I completely forgot."

His father frowned.

"Because I fell down the stairs." Linus could still picture the orange in his mind's eye, flying toward him in an arc. "I'll remember next time." He grinned. "Then I'll ask our Mr. Orange what his real name is."

He walked around behind his father and took a peek at the order book. "Mr. Orange," his father wrote in small, neat letters before adding the date and the amount.

Linus took his toothbrush from the bunch in the glass in the kitchen. Once again, the toothpaste was not where it should be. He finally found it in the wrong cupboard, without its cap.

As he brushed his teeth, he thought about the man with the sharp face and the painter's smock. He must be much older than his father, even though his father's black hair had turned gray a long time ago. Linus could still see the stern eyes that had started gleaming when the conversation turned to colors and puzzles. He had never met an adult who took playing so seriously. Why hadn't he told his mother and father more about Mr. Orange and his apartment full of colors?

Actually, I do know why I kept quiet, thought Linus. He looked all over the counter for the toothpaste cap and then in each of the cupboards. As long as he didn't tell anyone, it felt like he could keep the room all for himself.

He looked around. Now that he was back in his own home, which was full of bustle and voices, it was hard to picture Mr. Orange's white apartment. Had he really been in that quiet, white room? Here at home he could almost believe that he'd imagined the whole thing.

The cap had rolled under the kitchen table. Linus screwed it onto the tube and yawned. He walked down the hallway and quietly opened the bedroom door. For a moment, he felt confused as he stood there among the sleeping little ones, and he wondered what Max was doing in his bed. Then he smiled as he realized his mistake. He closed the door again, turned around and opened the door of his new bedroom.

"Colors of the future. That's interesting." Mister Superspeed is stretched out on Linus's bed, using his helmet as a pillow.

Linus nods. He sits down on the edge of the bed and pulls off his socks.

Mister Superspeed moves his helmet and folds his arms behind his head. "What was that other word he used for them?"

Linus shrugs. He's too tired to remember anything.

"Will you please get out of the way?" He pulls his pajamas from under the pillow, which isn't all that easy with Mister Superspeed lying on it. "I'm tired. I just want to go to sleep."

"What about me?"

"Go and rescue people. Win the war." Linus is yawning so much that his eyes have started to water.

Mister Superspeed puts on his helmet and sits up with a sigh. Linus's teary eyes blur the black and white of his costume into a gray haze.

Suddenly he realizes what Mister Superspeed is missing. Pencil lines aren't enough. A hero like him needs color. Strong color!

Linus sank back onto the bed. *A bright yellow helmet,* he thought dreamily. And a red costume, with blue boots and gloves. Or maybe the costume would be better in yellow, but then the helmet would have to be a different color… Linus slid beneath the covers and was out like a light.

7

Linus had secretly been hoping that his voice would become deeper when he moved into his new room. When he was still sleeping with the little ones he had often heard Albie's and Simon's voices rumbling away in their room, so low that he could never make out what they were saying. Linus had imagined that he and Simon would lie in bed talking like that, Simon up above and him down below.

But his voice stayed just the same after the move, and Simon still didn't say much to him. On Thursday evening, when Linus saw Mrs. De Winter on his list of Friday deliveries, he told Simon about what had happened with the garbage can on Monday.

"She always does that," said Simon. He was lying on the top bunk, staring up at the ceiling.

"So how did you deal with it?" asked Linus.

"Oh, you know." Simon turned to look at the wall.

He was equally tightlipped about his new job at the newspaper. *Maybe he misses Albie,* thought Linus, *and that's why he's so quiet.* But their mother said it was just his age.

"Albie was exactly the same," she said.

"Albie?" Linus's voice squeaked with surprise. His mother laughed.

"You were so little that you didn't notice," she told him. And she said it would be best to leave Simon alone.

Great, thought Linus. Then he'd just have to figure out what to do about Mrs. De Winter all by himself. When he heard the little ones laughing or squabbling, it almost made him long to be back in his old bedroom.

By the time he returned home from his round on Friday afternoon, it was already late. Mrs. De Winter had asked him to move a cupboard because her keys had fallen behind it. Linus had pushed the cupboard to one side, but the keys weren't there. Still, she wouldn't let him leave until he found the keys, which turned out to be buried between the sofa cushions.

As soon as he pushed his cart into the store, he could see from his mother's face that there was news. "Go take a look upstairs," she said with a smile. She had not looked so calm and relaxed all week.

A postcard from Albie was leaning against the vase on the table in the living room. Linus picked it up.

Dear everyone,

We have arrived safely at the training camp. We go on long marches every day and we all have blisters on our feet. The very first thing we learned was how to make our beds, with the sheets pulled so tight you can hardly get in. When I come back, I'll teach you all how to do it. Mom will be amazed! Letter to follow.

Love to you all from my very neat and tidy bed,
Your Albert

Before dinner, their father read out the postcard to the little ones, and they made him read it again after dinner. Willy and Sis kept begging him to read it again, read it again... They didn't stop until their father promised he would come and read it to them one last time when they were in bed.

When his father came back and sat down with the cashbook at the table opposite him, Linus looked up from his comic and took a deep breath.

"Why don't we have the blue star in our window yet?" He looked from his father to his mother, who was sitting in the easy chair with Albie's postcard in her hand. It looked as though she hadn't heard his question.

His father kept right on doing his accounts. Linus knew he wouldn't get an answer until his father had finished.

One of the neighbors had brought a pennant to Albie's farewell party. It was a sort of little flag—a white rectangle with a red border and a blue five-pointed star in the middle of the white. Every family with someone who had gone off to war was allowed to hang one of these pennants in their window. Linus looked for them and could spot them from a long way off. He thought they looked wonderful.

Finally his father wrote down a figure and turned the page.

"Would you like that?" he asked, as if Linus had asked him the question just a moment ago.

"Of course I would," said Linus. He thought it was a strange question. "Shouldn't everyone know that Albie's gone off to war?" He desperately wanted to hang up the pennant, so that everyone could see he had a brother who was a soldier. But

Albie had been gone almost a week now and the flag was still in the drawer of the sideboard.

His father looked at Linus and then at his mother.

"Flags are for celebrations. And wars are no cause for celebration." His mother spoke very quietly, the way she spoke when she was really angry. She didn't look up from the postcard.

All the same, Linus had to give it another try. "What Albie's doing is good, though, isn't it? Shouldn't we be proud of him?"

"War is nothing to be proud of. It's bad enough that it has to happen at all." His mother walked over and put Albie's postcard in the drawer of the sideboard, the drawer where the pennant was. Then she left the room without saying another word.

Linus groaned. He knew why his mother was angry. Not because Albie had joined the army, but because he had enlisted before they had called him up. He had signed up on his eighteenth birthday and had told the family only after he'd done it.

"I'd have been called up in a few weeks anyway," Albie had said.

"You have no way of knowing that!" That time she was so furious that she didn't bother to keep her voice down. "It might have been longer. Every day we have you safe here at home is a blessing."

"But I can't sit at home waiting when others are risking their lives!"

"I'm just saying that it makes no sense to go any sooner than necessary."

"But it *is* necessary. It's necessary *now!*" Albie had stood his ground. "The sooner this war is over, the better." That was Albie, always wanting to do the right thing. He always wanted to do the very best that he could. That's why Linus was so proud of him. That's why he wanted the blue star in the window.

He looked over at his father. Should he try again? He knew that he might have more luck with him.

But his father beat him to it. "You know what your mother thinks about this, son." He didn't look at Linus, just gave a little shrug and continued with his sums.

Linus didn't reply. He knew perfectly well that the war wasn't a cause for celebration, even without his mother reminding them of that every day. But he still could think that Albie was brave for going off to war, couldn't he?

Surely it wasn't wrong to be proud of your own brother?

8

AFTER TWO WEEKS OF deliveries, Linus was steering his cart between the pedestrians as though he had been doing it all his life. He whistled as he swerved around holes in the sidewalk and bumped up and down the curb without a single tomato or lemon escaping. He enjoyed being outside every afternoon, instead of sitting inside with the little ones. He felt free—even though, for now, he was still sticking very closely to the route that his father had mapped out for him.

Every Monday and Friday, he had to stop off at Mrs. De Winter's at the end of the afternoon. Today was also the Monday when he had to go to Mr. Orange's. It felt as though Mrs. De Winter could sense his impatience and intentionally kept him talking longer than usual. All the same, he didn't really mind doing chores for her and only half-listened to her complaints. *If I had to sit in that dreary apartment all day on my own I'd probably be in a grumpy mood too*, thought Linus as he finally climbed the stairs to Mr. Orange's apartment.

This time, the other door opened.

"Ah, my greengrocer! I was expecting you." Mr. Orange looked even thinner in his shirt and suspenders than in the baggy smock he had been wearing last time.

"Just put that down over there." He stepped aside to let Linus in and pointed at a small table in the middle of the kitchen. "How's your knee?"

"Fine," said Linus. "All mended." He put down the crate beside the table. It was the strangest table he had ever seen.

"Glad to hear it." Mr. Orange was silent for a moment as he looked pensively at the crate. "I still owe you an orange. I promise not to throw it at you this time. I can peel one for you if you like, or do you still have many more deliveries to make?"

Linus shook his head. "You're my last customer today."

"Ah, that's good. Please have a seat." Mr. Orange turned to the cupboard. Linus rested one hand on the table and couldn't resist taking a look underneath. The legs of the table were made of some kind of grooved slats, and there were even crossbars for the feet. It was painted white, just like the furniture in the bedroom.

"Made it myself," said Mr. Orange, putting two plates on the table. "Using a broken deckchair and pieces of wood from a canvas frame. They're called stretcher bars. They were too crooked to stretch a painting on, but they work pretty well as table legs, don't you think?"

"I think it's great…" Linus ran his hands over the legs. Everything about the table was simple, but he could tell that it had been made with care. Its thin legs made it look fragile, but it was actually very strong. *Just like Mr. Orange*, thought Linus.

"It's always fun to see what you can do with the things you happen to find around you," said Mr. Orange with a smile.

"My brother Albie often makes things himself," said Linus. "Actually, he's the one who built the delivery cart.

He took the wheels off our old baby carriage. So when my little sister was born, we had to push her around in the cart." He paused. "My brother's gone off to fight in the war."

Mr. Orange nodded, his attention on the orange. With a knife, he carefully divided it into two halves and then split the two halves again.

They sat in silence for a moment. The bustle of the city blew in through the window behind Linus. Cars honked and chugged at stoplights, while footsteps hurried to overtake one another. The activity outside made it seem even quieter inside. Linus leaned back and watched the slender hands cutting the quarters in two. The scent of orange was all around them.

"Why is it that smells don't have names?" Linus spoke without thinking.

Mr. Orange was using the knife to remove the pieces of peel. He didn't answer, but his eyebrows twitched upward slightly. He lined up eight little orange boats across the plate.

"Like colors," Linus continued. "There's pale blue, sky blue, navy blue, but there are no words for smells."

"You're right." Mr. Orange placed the orange on the plate and pushed it toward Linus. He picked up the second orange and started again. Halves, quarters, eighths. Linus chewed a piece of orange. The silence went on for so long that he started to feel nervous.

"Questions like that always make my father sigh," he blurted out. "He says I shouldn't ask questions that don't have an answer."

"Of course you should!" Mr. Orange waved the knife as though it was his forefinger. "Just because you don't immediately have an answer doesn't mean it's not a good question. It just means that you have to go looking for the answer. And looking for an answer that's new... Well, that's something you have to take your time about. In fact, it's a very good question." Mr. Orange was looking so intently at him that Linus felt a little uncomfortable. He quickly put the last piece of orange into his mouth and pulled the delivery list from his pocket.

"My father wants to know your real name." He tried to smooth out the piece of paper. "We couldn't read it on the order form."

"My real name?" His eyebrows shot up above the top of his glasses.

Linus hesitated for a moment. "We've been calling you Mr. Orange," he confessed. He put his list down on the table. Mr. Orange started to laugh. His face looked a lot happier now.

"That's not my first nickname, you know," he said, taking the piece of paper. "My brother calls me Sleepy."

Sleepy? Linus couldn't see anything sleepy about him.

"I love to paint deep into the night." Mr. Orange smiled at the look of surprise on Linus's face. "And that means I get up late, too. Sleepy is one of the dwarfs in *Snow White*. Did you see the movie? It's entirely animated and absolutely enormous! I've been back to see it many times."

Linus shook his head. "I've seen some other cartoons," he said. "About Superman. He's a comic book superhero who comes from another planet. He..." Linus paused. "He wears your colors."

"My colors?" Mr. Orange cocked his head.

"The strong colors... from the room I saw last time?" Linus could feel himself starting to blush. Suddenly he was scared that he'd imagined it after all.

"Ah, the primary colors, you mean." Mr. Orange took a pencil from his jacket pocket. "They're called that because you can use them to mix every other color. But I like to use them just as they are."

Linus leaned forward enthusiastically. "My brother Albie's good at drawing. He's even invented his own superhero who fights against evil. Against the war."

"Against the waaaar…" Mr. Orange drew out the last word. "That's good."

Linus nodded. "When my brother comes back, I'm going to tell him about the strong colors. I think his hero could use them. He's called Mister Superspeed."

Mr. Orange wrote something on the list and slid it back across the table to Linus. "And what's your name, by the way?" Linus told him.

"Nice to meet you, Linus." He stood up and pretended to take off his hat to Linus. Linus picked up the paper and stood up too.

"Nice to meet you…" He looked at the name on the paper. It was going to be difficult to pronounce.

"… Mr. Orange." He stopped, with his hand on the door handle, and looked back. "That name suits you better." Then, feeling suddenly shy, he opened the door and dashed down the stairs. His shoes made a lot of noise, so he wasn't sure if he really heard Mr. Orange laughing or if he was just imagining things.

9

"We need to think of a present for Lizzy," said Linus's mother that evening to his father, who was sitting at the table bringing the cashbook up to date. She was mending the hem of a dress. Their mother was the only one who ever used Sissie's real name. It was Sis's birthday on Sunday.

"Bertie?" She looked up from her work. "Did you hear what I said?"

His father was tallying things up.

Linus lowered his comic book. He thought about the shop beneath Mr. Orange's apartment. ANTIQUES AND CURIOSITIES, it said above the door. Last week he had seen a little music box on display in the window. It was lined with shiny white silk. In the middle was a tiny doll that pirouetted round and round, just like Sis when she danced. She would arch her arms above her head and spin in circles until she got dizzy. And whenever she fell over, she was always the one who laughed loudest.

As Linus had stood gazing into the window, the woman inside the shop had walked over to the display. It was nearly closing time. She carefully shut the lid of the music box. As she did so, she looked out at Linus as though they were sharing a secret; as though they were the only ones in the world who knew that there was something special inside that ordinary-looking wooden box.

"I might have an idea for Sis's present," said Linus. His mother sat up and looked at him in surprise. Even his father glanced up from his cashbook.

"You're a funny one, Linus Muller," his mother said the next day as they stood together in front of the shop window. She gave him a strange look, like she could suddenly see something different about him. They walked into the store and asked about the music box. His mother looked shocked when she heard the price, but then she took out her change purse.

"It's because you're the one who found it for Lizzy," she said with a wink. "And because it's the perfect present for her. Let's make it a gift from all of us."

10

Dear Sis,

Happy, happy second birthday! I chose this card just for you. I hope you have the best birthday ever. Too bad I can't be there with you!

Everything here is fine and dandy. I've already learned how to put together a gun in just under a minute. We've done so many push-ups and sit-ups that I've lost count. I'm getting muscles like Superman! It's all so quiet and peaceful out here in the woods that you could think you're on vacation. And if the food didn't remind us that we're in the army, we could almost forget there's a war going on. They say we'll be off to Europe sooner than planned, but maybe that's just a rumor.

Have an extra piece of birthday cake for me, Sis. And make it a big one!

Love, Albert

There was a picture of a war ship on the front of the postcard. Sis had decided she was going to take it everywhere with her all day. She showed it to everyone who came to visit, until the card was so crumpled that their father had to take it away and put it on the sideboard where she couldn't reach it.

After that, the music box had her full attention. Whenever she opened the lid, the tune would start to play again. And again. The more it repeated, the more annoying it became. Linus was starting to regret his bright idea.

He looked longingly out of the window. The afternoon was nearly over but he had not been outside all day. He had seen the latest issue of *Action Comics* at the newsstand yesterday, and he couldn't wait to go and buy it. When the bell rang and another unexpected visitor arrived, he used the opportunity to slip outside. He heaved a sigh of relief. First he'd go and see if Liam was at home. If so, they could go to the newsstand together.

"How's Albie doing?" Rosie asked as Linus was waiting for Liam to untangle his shoelaces. It seemed as though she wasn't being quite so mean to him lately. That must be because he had a brother in the army now.

"We just got some news from him." Linus waited for a moment, trying to build up the tension. "He can put his gun together and take it apart in just under a minute."

"His gun?" Rosie's eyes widened.

"What do you think they use? Broomsticks?" Liam finally had his shoes on. "In less than a minute?" he asked, as he pulled Linus to the front door.

Linus nodded. He was glowing with pride. "In the pitch dark, too," he quickly added, so that Rosie would hear it before the door closed behind them. Whenever he spoke about Albie, the words often came out differently from how he had intended.

But even if what I said about the dark isn't true right now, Linus thought as he ran down the stairs after Liam, *Albie's sure to be able to do that soon, and then it won't be a lie.*

"Did you ask about Halloween yet?" Liam gave Linus a shove and ran ahead. "It's next Monday."

"Yes, it's fine!" He'd completely forgotten about it. They went trick or treating together every year, but Linus had always had to drag the little ones along. This year was the first time they were allowed to go alone, just the two of them. Linus had pestered his mother until she had promised to take the little ones herself this year.

The comic was already sold out at the newsstand on Second Avenue. "Since the war started, we just can't seem to get enough of them," the newspaper seller said with a smile. They ran to the corner of Park Avenue, where the newsstand still had some copies. Linus took one and paid with Albie's money. The two boys sat down on a bench.

The cover had a picture of an American soldier who was driving a motorbike right through the firing line. Superman was flying alongside him. He had caught a grenade in his bare hand.

"About Halloween…" Liam was still panting. "Do you mind if Rosie comes with us?"

Rosie wanted to go with them? Linus gave Liam a sideways glance. "You're kidding, right?"

"Yeah, I know. It's a pain," said Liam apologetically. He had misunderstood Linus's question. "But my dad made me promise."

"Fine by me." Linus tried to sound like he didn't care.

"Okay." Liam jumped to his feet, looking relieved. "Hey, I've got to run."

"What time are we going out?" Linus called after him. Liam shouted something back, but his words were lost in the crowd. *I was right*, thought Linus, *she has been acting differently since I've had a brother in the army*! He rolled up his comic and stood up. Next Monday suddenly seemed a very long way off.

11

"Delivery!"

Mr. Orange's kitchen door stood wide open. Linus put down the crate and peered around the door.

"Linus!" Mr. Orange's head appeared in the opposite doorway. He waved for him to come in. "Come and see what I've made with your boxes."

Linus walked through the kitchen, but stopped short in the doorway, staring straight ahead. The bare wooden floor stretched out in front of him. The room was almost entirely empty, with just a stool or table here and there against the wall. Sunlight streamed in through three large windows. It reflected off the polished floor and seemed to bounce back at him from the white walls.

Wherever he looked, he saw colored shapes, even more than in the other room. Big and small, on their own and in groups, like clouds of color. Linus took a few steps. He felt as though everything around him was moving. *And yet*, he thought in surprise, *it's so peaceful.*

"Not bad, you think?" Mr. Orange stood beside a small white cupboard, with one hand on his hip, a cigarette in the other. "It's perfect for my tubes of paint and palette knives." He gave the side of the cupboard a contented pat.

It took Linus a moment to recognize his own orange crates. Mr. Orange had joined them together and added shelves. He had arranged jars of paintbrushes on top of the cabinet, with the bristles pointing upward, like strange bouquets of flowers.

"I think I'm finally getting this place organized." Mr. Orange walked to the middle of the room and spun around. Then he looked at Linus, his head cocked to the side. "So, what do you think? How's it looking?"

Linus struggled to find the right words to describe it. "It's so… lively," he said. "It's almost like a dance hall."

Mr. Orange laughed, delighted. "A dance hall for painting in," he said, rubbing his hands together. "Well, I think that calls for some music!"

He walked over to a small table with a red box on it and lifted the lid to reveal a record player. All Linus's family had at home was a radio, but Liam's father had a record player, and he liked to listen to opera on Sunday afternoons. The women's voices sang so high that it gave Linus goose bumps whenever he heard them.

"You know, in the future everyone will be able to live like this." Mr. Orange held his cigarette in the corner of his mouth and carefully shook a gleaming black record from its sleeve.

"Everyone?" Linus's eyes widened. "Like this? So… so… bright and cheerful?"

Mr. Orange smiled. "Do you like the sound of that?" He took the cigarette from his mouth, blew a few specks of dust from the record, and placed it on the turntable.

"In the future, everything will be different. Take paintings—they'll be old-fashioned by then." He nodded at a row of paintings leaning against the wall. Linus could see only the backs of them, with their wooden frames. Stretcher bars, as he now knew they were called.

"If you make sure that the things around you are a good match and also suit the room they are in, then the whole room becomes more attractive. Or more bright and cheerful, as you say. And then you don't need any individual paintings."

Linus looked around at the colored squares in the sunlight. They were like splashes of paint on a painting, but a giant painting that you could walk around in.

"It's like the whole room is a painting…" Then he thought about the other room. "I mean the whole apartment!"

"Nicely put." Mr. Orange held the needle above the record. "And why stop at one apartment? Maybe in the future we can make the entire city into one big painting. A painting where everything is constantly changing." He clapped his hands. "Orange?"

The music started before Linus could answer. Mr. Orange walked ahead of him into the kitchen. As he walked, he did a funny kind of skip, so quickly that Linus wasn't sure that he'd actually seen it. "Have you heard this music before? It's boogie-woogie, the very latest thing. This is the music of the future!"

Linus tried to imagine a city of the future, a city with Mr. Orange's colors and with this kind of music. Bright, cheerful music that even had a funny name. Music that suited the colors and made the shapes on the walls dance. Music that made everyone dance. *If Mr. Orange's future looks like this*, thought Linus as he followed him, *then I hope it comes soon.*

Two plates were already waiting on the kitchen table, with a knife beside them.

"They're good for me, these oranges." Mr. Orange took two oranges from the new crate, stubbed out his cigarette and coughed. "Anyone who smokes as much as I do needs to eat lots and lots of fruit." He sliced an orange in half.

Linus watched for the smile on Mr. Orange's face. Maybe it was there, at the corner of his mouth, but he wasn't sure. It was hard to tell when he was making a joke. As if performing an operation, Mr. Orange cut the halves in two again, just as precisely as he had the last time. At the same moment, he flapped his elbows in and out to the beat of the music. It was a strange, stiff movement, and it reminded Linus of a penguin. To keep himself from laughing, he looked the other way, through the open door and into the studio.

"If people won't need paintings in the future," he asked, "what will you do?"

"Oh, that's not going to happen for a long time!" Mr. Orange pointed his knife at something that was far away. "For now, it's all about looking. Experimenting. Constantly trying out new things." He shrugged his shoulders.

Linus thought about the nail holes in the walls. You could see from all those tiny holes just how hard Mr. Orange had been looking. Linus watched the slender fingers as they pulled apart the little boats of orange, one by one. How much longer would Mr. Orange's search take?

"I don't think it's something I'll ever see myself," said Mr. Orange, as though he could hear Linus's thoughts. "But maybe you'll be around to see it, when you're a grown-up."

"A grown-up?" exclaimed Linus. He was going to have to wait a really long time. "But that means you've worked all this time for nothing, doesn't it?"

"Absolutely not!" Mr. Orange didn't seem to mind the question. His eyes sparkled behind the thick frame of his glasses. "This kind of thing is a long, long process. It started before I was born and it will continue when I'm gone. You need lots and lots of people to make it work—that's the marvelous thing about it!"

The music stopped, and the doorbell rang just at that moment, as if the person who rang the bell had waited politely for the record to finish.

"Ah, my visitor." Mr. Orange went out into the hallway to greet his guest. Linus heard the door downstairs spring open, followed by footsteps hurrying up the stairs.

"Linus, this is my friend Harry. He's taking me out for dinner." His last word ended in a coughing fit. The man called Harry patted him gently on the back. He was much younger than Mr. Orange.

"Harry," he continued when he'd finished coughing, "meet Linus, the young man who keeps me healthy. He delivers the best oranges in all of New York, and he calls me Mr. Orange. Isn't that a good joke?"

"It certainly is. Particularly when you consider that your Mr. Orange would never paint with orange," said Harry to Linus.

"And not only that." Mr. Orange's eyes sparkled. "He also asks the best questions in all of New York." Mr. Orange picked up a piece of peel from the table. "Linus would like to know, for instance, why there are no words for smells." He placed the peel in Harry's hand. "We're looking for a name for the scent of an orange. What would you say?"

"I would say… that it is indeed a very good question." Harry winked at Linus.

Linus laughed a little shyly. "I have to go home," he said, standing up.

Harry shook him firmly by the hand. "Good work, Linus. Keep it up."

Linus nodded. He didn't know whether Harry meant that he should deliver more oranges or think up more questions.

"See you next time." Mr. Orange pointed at his smock. "I now must go in search of my evening attire." He pursed his lips, pronouncing the last two words snootily. Linus smiled. Then he waved and headed downstairs. He moved slowly because his head felt so heavy with all the things he'd just seen and heard. He didn't want all of his new thoughts to get tangled up. He wanted to hang on to them so that he could take them out later and explore them from lots of different angles.

12

At home, there was no room at all for his new thoughts. Sis was crying non-stop because she was not allowed to open her music box while they were eating. Willy and Max were fighting over Willy's tin soldiers, which they always played with together. Willy said that Max had hidden them. Max yelled that he was the biggest and the boss and that the boss really didn't need to steal silly little soldiers.

After dinner, Linus escaped to his bedroom. He sat on the edge of his bed. Someone slammed a door. Willy screamed. Sis whined. The bright, cheerful feeling of that afternoon felt very far away.

Linus shrugged and lay back on his bed. Something was sticking into his back. He reached under the blanket and pulled out a tin soldier. How many times had he and Simon told Max and Willy they weren't allowed to play in their room? He marched back into the living room and slammed the soldier down on the table in front of Willy. At least that stopped his yelling, but then Sissie took the silence as an invitation to start wailing all over again.

Linus went back to lie on his bed. He turned onto his side and stared at the wallpaper. It was the same wallpaper as everywhere else in the house. Before he'd visited Mr. Orange, he'd never paid any attention to it. Now he could suddenly see just how loud and busy the pattern of dark green leaves and red flowers was.

In the future, everyone will be able to live like this. Maybe you'll be around to see it, Mr. Orange had said.

Simon came bursting into the bedroom and slammed the door behind him.

"Hey," said Linus, sitting up. "I have an idea for brightening up the place. We should ask if we can paint the walls white."

"Paint them white?" Simon pulled a face, like there was a bad smell in the room. He aimed his jacket at the hook on the back of the door. "What's the point? This isn't a hospital." The jacket hit the door and landed in a crumpled pile on the floor. Simon stood on Linus's mattress and swung up onto his own bunk. The bed creaked and Linus shook with every movement.

"It'll make the room a lot brighter, so it'll seem bigger." Linus hesitated. Should he tell Simon about Mr. Orange?

"What a dumb idea. What good is it if the room just *seems* bigger?" Simon flopped onto his bed. The mattress sagged in the middle and Linus just managed to lie back down in time to get out of the way.

"But let me know if you manage to come up with a plan for actually *making* it bigger, okay?" Simon held out his socks and dropped them to the floor. One of them landed on Linus's bunk. He picked it up with two fingers and threw it as far away as he could.

Albie would think it was a good idea, thought Linus. He rolled over onto his side so that he didn't have to look at the mess. He would have been able to tell Albie all about Mr. Orange.

When he closed his eyes, he could see the colored shapes floating through his mind. He imagined Sis's crying becoming quieter and quieter, and the smell of Simon's socks fading away.

13

"We got mail!" Willy stood at the top of the stairs, waving his battleaxe. His Indian headdress had slipped down over one eye.

"From Albie?" Linus looked over at his father, who was talking to a customer in the store. *All right, you can go up and take a quick look*, his eyes said.

Linus put the cart in its usual place and ran upstairs. It was Monday, Halloween, and he had come home late. Mrs. De Winter had made him move the cupboard because she'd lost her keys yet again. It was almost five o'clock by the time Linus finally found them, this time under a different cupboard.

"Here. You can read it yourself." His mother handed him the letter, but the little ones screamed for him to read it out loud.

Dear Mom and Dad, Sis and brothers,
  A late-night message from me to let you know that we're off. In fact, we're going earlier than planned. As I write this letter, I'm not far from home. I'm sitting in the back of an army truck and we're hurtling in a convoy through Brooklyn,

on our way to the terminal where the boats are waiting. We're making a real racket! I don't think anyone in Brooklyn is going to get a wink of sleep until the war is over. We'll be boarding the ship in a couple of hours. By the time you all get up (except for Dad, of course, who'll have been out of bed for hours by then), we'll already be at sea.

I'm thinking of you all.

In haste, with lots of love, Albert

PS Thanks, Mom, for the cake, from me and some of the other guys. It was so good it was almost a danger to our health. A couple of us very nearly gobbled up our fingers too!

"He's going for real, he's going for real!" Willy tried to pull his headdress straight while waving his battleaxe around at the same time. Max held his black magician's cape up above his head, making it billow out behind him as he ran around the room. He'd abandoned the matching top hat on a chair. For years, Linus had been the magician. He could still remember how the hat had chafed his ears.

He's going for real, thought Linus. His brother was on a ship, on his way to Europe. He stared at Willy and Max, who were chasing each other around the table. He couldn't imagine what it must be like for Albie.

"Abbie, Abbie!" Sis was dancing on top of the table. Their mother was trying to get Sis's little feet into her bunny suit, but she had to give up and wait until Sis had finished dancing around. She raised her eyebrows and smiled at Linus. It was a thin smile.

"Quickly, you," she said to him, glancing at the clock. It was almost half past five. Linus took a look in the dress-up box. He had the choice of pirate or cowboy.

CHAPTER 13

It was already getting dark outside. Linus pushed the pirate hat onto his head and tried to tie the strings of his eye patch as he ran. He still hadn't managed to do them up by the time he reached Liam's house. The door opened before he could ring the bell, and a wolf's head peered out, eyes bulging.

"You're so late!" Liam's voice sounded hollow inside the mask.

"We just got a letter. From Albie," said Linus. "They're on their way to Europe." It still sounded so strange to him.

"Europe! Do you think he'll go to Paris?" asked Rosie. She was wearing a witch's hat with a mask and a wig. The mask had a hooked nose and witch's teeth. He could just see Rosie's own mouth inside the mask, so it looked like she had two rows of teeth. One row was higgledy-piggledy and the other was nice and straight.

"It's not a vacation. There's a war on. Remember?" the wolf said, shaking its head.

"They're in the middle of the ocean now." Linus handed Liam the eye patch and turned around so he could tie it on for him.

"Is that why you're wearing your little sailor suit?" Georgie MacKenna followed Rosie outside. "Maybe we can find a rowboat so you can go after him." Georgie went and stood beside Rosie, with his hands in his pockets, and smirked at Linus as though he'd just said something really clever.

"You're one to talk, Georgie. You're not even wearing a costume." Rosie gave him a shove, but she still laughed.

"Don't need one. I'm scary enough all by myself!" MacKenna growled and made his fingers into claws. Rosie ran away screaming, with MacKenna chasing after her.

"What's *he* doing here?" Linus said, punching Liam's arm.

"I told you Rosie was coming, didn't I?" Liam had pushed up his mask so that he could see better. "Mom and Dad said she couldn't go out on her own with him."

"You said *Rosie* was coming." Linus glared at him. "You didn't say anything about MacKenna."

Georgie MacKenna was almost the same age as Simon, but he'd been held back for two years at school, so now he was in Rosie's class. He was one of the meanest boys in the school. Linus couldn't understand why Rosie would want to have anything to do with him.

"What was I supposed to do?" Liam tried to take Linus's arm and pull him along. "I couldn't exactly say no, could I?"

"Well, to start with, you could have told me," said Linus, tugging his arm away.

"And would you still have come?" asked Liam.

Like that was any excuse! "Of course not!" Linus snapped. He didn't know at whom he was more angry—Liam for not saying anything, or himself for being so stupid and thinking that Rosie might want to go with the two of them. He suddenly felt really dumb, with his pirate hat and his eye patch.

"Don't worry about it! Just ignore them," said Liam. "Hey, and remember, I had to sit in there with that idiot for an hour waiting for you because you were so stupidly late."

"Serves you right." Linus tried to return Liam's angry look, but it wasn't easy with just one eye. Liam burst out laughing, and suddenly Linus couldn't quite remember why he had been so angry. He gave Liam an extra-hard shove, and they ran off to catch up with the others.

The streets were busy. Other small groups of children were going from door to door like them, and soldiers were wandering among them, going from bar to bar. Maybe they were on leave. Or perhaps they were waiting for a ship to take them to Europe.

The gang got a treat at nearly every door they knocked on and their bags were soon bulging with candy and fruit. Rosie and MacKenna were falling farther and farther behind. Liam was right—it was best just to ignore them.

Linus and Liam rang an old man's doorbell, but when they said "Trick or treat?" he just wandered back into his house and left the door open. They looked at each other, shrugged their shoulders, and stood there waiting. After about a minute, Liam called out, "Hello? Trick or treat?" By the time the old man finally came back to the front door, the other two had caught up with them. Bold as ever, MacKenna stuck out his hand. The man gave each of them two small pears.

"Aw, these things are rock hard," said Georgie before the man had even shut the door. He took a bite and spat it right out. "Horrors," he shouted. "Poison pears!"

"They're cooking pears," snapped Linus. "You can't eat them raw."

The door from a bar opened onto the street. A witch with a haystack of hair came barreling out, screeching with laughter, a soldier on each arm. She was followed by a monster with an ax stuck in his head, who was tugging along a nurse wearing a uniform covered in red stains. Then came another soldier and a man in a Superman costume, with their arms around each other's shoulders. The Superman outfit was far too small for the man. A seam had burst at his waist, revealing his white undershirt beneath.

"Come on. Let's go over there!" The monster with the ax reeled across the street. The others followed.

"Hey, Superman!" Georgie MacKenna pulled back his arm and threw the pear that he'd taken a bite of. "See if you can protect yourself from this!" The first pear missed its target, but the second one hit him on the back. The man stopped in the middle of the street and turned around. He put up his fists and threw a few punches in their direction. A car honked as it swerved around him. Georgie grabbed another pear from Liam's hand and aimed again. This time the man tried to catch it, but the pear hit him right in the chest.

"I surrender!" Smiling, the man put his hands up and walked off with his friends. Georgie waved his fist, as though he'd actually won some kind of contest, and he pulled Rosie along after him.

"That Superman shouldn't have given in like that," Linus said as he watched the man disappear into a bar on the other side of the street. He dropped his pears into his bag. "Someone like him doesn't deserve to wear that costume."

Liam put his arm around Linus's shoulders. "Hey, how about we have a bit of fun now, Linus Muller?"

Linus shrugged. *If it had been Mister Superspeed*, he thought as Liam dragged him off, *he'd have put that Georgie MacKenna in his place.* He was sure of that!

14

Linus had to ring twice before the door buzzed open and he could pull the cart inside. When he had first started making his deliveries, he had thought a crate of oranges weighed a ton, but now he could carry one upstairs easily. He knocked on the kitchen door and waited. There was a lot of bumping and banging before the door slowly opened.

"Hello, Linus." Mr. Orange was wearing pajamas with dark-red stripes. Over his pajamas, he wore an elegant black jacket. It made a funny-looking outfit. He looked tired and Linus could see the stubble on his cheeks. One of his cheeks was badly swollen.

"Inflammation," said Mr. Orange, pointing at it. "Went to the dentist yesterday." His *s*'s sounded funny.

"I'm still feeling poorly so I'd better not ask you in." He took an orange from the crate, which Linus was still holding.

"I hope you feel better soon," said Linus, putting the crate down by the door.

"It'll get better, slowly but surely." Mr. Orange tried to smile. "Don't forget about these!" he said, holding up the orange. He walked with Linus to the top of the stairs and watched him go.

"By the way, how is your brother doing?" he suddenly asked when Linus was already halfway down the stairs. "Have you heard from him again?"

"He's on his way to Europe," Linus called upstairs. "On a ship."

"That's a long journey," said Mr. Orange, leaning on the stair rail. "I've done it, too. But in the opposite direction, from England."

Linus stopped walking.

"Three years ago. Just after the war started."

"What was it like on the ship?" Linus took a few steps up the stairs. "Was there a swimming pool on board?" Before the war, he and Liam sometimes used to go and take a look at the ocean steamers when they docked in the Hudson. Gazing up at the ships and their many decks, stacked one on top of another, they had felt like tiny ants. Linus had once seen a poster with pictures of a ship that had a swimming pool on the top deck and he thought they all might be that way.

"A swimming pool?" Mr. Orange frowned. "I don't remember there being a swimming pool. And if there was one, they'd have used it for storage. The ship was packed. And no one was thinking about swimming, anyway."

"Why not?" Linus thought a swimming pool in the middle of the ocean would be fantastic. It seemed such a pity to miss out on a chance like that.

"We had other things on our minds." Mr. Orange looked as though he was surprised that Linus had to ask. "Most of all, we were frightened."

"Frightened?" Suddenly Linus began to feel worried. He climbed back up a few more steps.

"Of being attacked." Mr. Orange sat down on the top step.

"The enemy sent out submarines to search the entire ocean for our ships. They call them U-boats."

Linus nodded. He knew all about U-boats from the comic strips about the war. Albie had made a good drawing of one, too.

"So we traveled in a convoy, with as many ships as possible. It was our only protection against attacks." Mr. Orange seemed to have forgotten about the pain in his cheek. Linus sat down beside him. He'd never considered that the crossing might be dangerous.

"It was especially tense at night. We had to sail with a blackout, in complete darkness, so that we didn't give ourselves away to the enemy." Mr. Orange sat staring straight ahead, as though he could see through the wall and into the distance, toward the horizon.

"I sat up on deck, day and night, because I was suffering from seasickness." He glanced sideways at Linus. "It was cloudy most of the time. And that meant that it was pitch black out at sea. No stars, no moon, no horizon, nothing to fix your eyes on. After a while it was impossible to tell which way was up and which was down." His smile looked a little sad. Or maybe it was just his swollen cheek.

"The sound of the sea, the wind blowing through your hair, and the endless thumping of the engines… That's all there was. Night after night after night."

Linus held his breath.

"The strange thing was that we knew there were other ships sailing close by. During the daytime we could see them. But at night, in the dark, we felt as though we were all alone." He shook his head. "When the moon came out, we could see the crests of the waves. They looked like bright white lines. And sometimes we'd see the outline of another ship suddenly looming up in the darkness. It always surprised me how close they were." He took a deep breath and released it slowly. "The crossing seemed to go on forever and ever…"

They sat in silence for a while.

"But the U-boats never found your ship?" Linus asked finally.

"No. Thank goodness!" Mr. Orange sounded as relieved as if he had just stepped off the ship onto solid ground. He took the stair rail and slowly pulled himself to his feet.

"Still, every day since I've arrived, I've felt so happy that I took that chance. I wouldn't want to have missed out on everything here!" He spread his arms and his black jacket fell loosely around him. "New York is a city you can be proud of." He looked at Linus. "You're so lucky you were born here."

"Do you think so?" Linus stood up. He'd never seen it that way himself.

"New York is the city of the future," declared Mr. Orange, as though it were perfectly obvious. "When the war is over, the whole world will be different. Better than ever before. I'm certain of that. And in a modern city like this, you'll notice it first. In fact, I can feel it happening already."

He put his hand on Linus's shoulder. "By fighting, your brother is helping to make this future possible. That's another reason to be proud."

Giving Linus a wave, Mr. Orange headed back into his apartment and closed the door.

Linus walked downstairs. He had been proud of Albie all along, but after hearing Mr. Orange's story there was another word that was trying to sneak into his thoughts. A word he didn't want to let in. As he left the building, he shut the door behind him with a bang—as though that might scare the word away.

15

Whenever Simon turned over on the top bunk, Linus's bottom bunk shook too. He hadn't been able to sleep all night. The story Mr. Orange had told him that afternoon kept running through his head.

Mr. Orange had come to New York to escape the war. Albie had left to fight in Europe. *It's as if they changed places*, he thought. Maybe Albie was even on Mr. Orange's ship right now.

Light seeped in through the gap in the curtain, the electrical light of the city that was always there, clouds or no clouds. Linus could see the outline of the bed above him, as well as Simon's jacket, heaped on the floor, with his own bag beside it.

He needed it to be darker. He pulled the covers over his head. Now, when he blinked, there was no difference between having his eyes open or closed. He put his fingers in his ears to block out the sound of his father's snoring, which was coming through the thin wall.

Maybe Albie was sitting on the deck now in the dark. Maybe he was lying on his back and searching the sky for stars. Linus tried to imagine that he was lying next to Albie, which made him feel calmer. When he held his breath, he could almost hear the waves crashing onto the bow of the ship. If he focused hard enough, he could almost see the first stars…

But it's just started to hail. What a shame! It really stings, too. How can Albie sleep through that? But wait, now that the moon has come out, he can see that it's not hail at all. It's little tin soldiers falling down from the sky with their pointed bayonets at the ready. He will have to fight! Fight for the future! He waves his arms around wildly. If the future's at stake, where's Mister Superspeed?

"I'm over here. But I'm busy right now!" Mister Superspeed is sitting beside a swimming pool, dangling his legs over the edge. In his white underwear, he's easy to see in the moonlight. His costume is lying in his lap.

"What are you doing? You're not mending your costume at a moment like this, are you?"

"My uniform," says Mister Superspeed, correcting him. "Those nasty little soldiers have pricked tiny holes all over it and the seam has come undone at the waist."

"That's not important right now. It's the future that's at stake!"

"Well, the future can wait just a little bit longer." Mister Superspeed sews with small, neat stitches. "I have to keep up my appearance. How am I supposed to put other people in their place if I look like a slob?" He proudly holds up his uniform. The yellow fabric glows in the moonlight. His blue gloves look almost green.

The moon disappears behind a cloud. But why does it feel so stuffy? He can hardly breathe. He can barely even move. The more he struggles to free himself, the more trapped he feels. He's getting warmer and warmer.

"Stop wriggling around!" *Who said that? Now that his arms are finally free, he can breathe again. Suddenly there's light. Far too much light! Light is dangerous.*

"Careful! There's a blackout!" *He kicks his legs free.*

"Okay, okay. I'll turn off the light if you keep the noise down." Strange that Mister Superspeed's voice sounds so much like Simon's. The light's so bright he can't see anything at all.

It took Linus a moment to figure out that the dark shape above him was Simon's head. For a second, he thought Simon was smiling, but that was because his head was hanging upside down.

"Keep the noise down! You'll wake everyone up," the head said angrily.

"I was having a nightmare," said Linus. His heart was pounding and he was completely tangled up in his sheets.

"Well, don't!" said Simon. Then his head disappeared and the light went out.

Linus freed his legs from the sheets. He felt around beneath the bed for his flashlight and Albie's sketchbook, which he'd been looking through earlier. He pulled the sheet over his head. By the dim glow of the flashlight, he leafed through the pages until he came to the drawing of a U-boat. Mister Superspeed hovered over it. Little steam clouds kept him up in the air. He was tying a knot in the steel tube of the periscope, which stuck up out of the submarine. The drawing of the knot was a bit messy but it was still clear that the knot had done its job. The ocean steamer, which was just visible on the horizon, was now safe to continue on its way.

How long would it take Albie to cross the ocean? Linus felt dumb for not having asked Mr. Orange. Now he had no idea when they might expect to hear from him again.

It felt stuffy under the covers. Linus switched off the flashlight and pushed back the blanket. He could breathe again, but he still couldn't shake the anxious feeling that had come over him.

16

"No news is good news," their neighbor Mrs. Hensen said every day. Whenever the mailman came by, she always happened to drop in after to buy a little something. Two tomatoes, an onion, a little sprig of parsley. And then, casually, she would ask if there was any news from Albie.

Now, whenever she saw Mrs. Hensen coming, Linus's mother would disappear upstairs and send someone else down to help out in the store. On the afternoons when Linus was already at home, he was the one who had to wrap up a leek in newspaper for her or weigh half a pound of tomatoes and tell her that there'd been no news that day.

"Maybe tomorrow," she'd say as she left the store.

"Maybe tomorrow," Linus would repeat politely.

One day, when he went back upstairs, he found his mother staring out of the window.

"That woman is starting to get on my nerves," she said. She was pulling at the fingers of one hand with the other, going from her pinky to her thumb and back again. Linus nodded. He too was finding it hard to cope with the long wait for news.

Maybe tomorrow.

But they still hadn't received any news from Albie by the next time he went to Mr. Orange's. *Almost three weeks*, thought Linus as he climbed the stairs. He wanted to hear more about Mr. Orange's ocean crossing, so he was glad that he had been able to make it there early. He hadn't needed to stop at Mrs. De Winter's, since his father had told him that she was in the hospital.

He could already hear music coming through the door. The music with the funny name. What had Mr. Orange called it? He would have to ask him. He knocked on the door. Then he heard quick footsteps coming closer and someone laughing a high-pitched laugh. The door swung open.

"Linus!" Mr. Orange's voice sounded almost jolly. He was wearing a handsome black suit, and he made an elegant little bow that seemed to go with it. Linus recognized the jacket as the one Mr. Orange had been wearing over his pajamas the last time he saw him. There was no sign of the swollen cheek now.

With a flourish, he picked up an orange and handed it to Linus. "I have a visitor this afternoon, so I hope you'll forgive me for not peeling it." Then he leaned over to whisper confidentially, "It's a lady who wants to buy my paintings. A journalist!" His eyes were gleaming.

"I'll see you next time." He put his thumb up and before Linus could say anything, the door was already closing and Mr. Orange and his crate had disappeared inside.

Linus walked slowly down the stairs. He still didn't know how long Mr. Orange's ship had taken to reach New York. A feeling of deep disappointment came over him as he pulled his cart through the gate. It was a dark afternoon. When he looked up at Mr. Orange's, he saw that the lights were already on inside. The windows on the second floor were warm yellow squares. If he listened carefully, he could still hear the music above the sounds of the street.

Suddenly he remembered what the music was called. Boogie-woogie.

When Linus got home, it was his mother who opened the door for him. The moment he saw her big smile, he knew exactly what it meant.

"Mail?" he asked breathlessly. She shrugged and said nothing, but he could tell from her eyes that he had guessed right. Upstairs there was an atmosphere of joyful anticipation. The envelope was leaning against the vase on the sideboard. Linus picked it up to take a look. It was a fat one this time. He ran his finger over the neat letters and put down the envelope with a contented sigh.

Finally, when the store was closed and everyone was sitting around the table, their father carefully opened the envelope.

Dear everyone,

After ten days on a packed ship, we have arrived in Italy. We were all so happy to get off the ship at long last. Now that I can stretch my legs and sleep better, I feel fine. Most of the others are just as happy as I am that the waiting's finally over and things are really starting. It's so much better than just waiting. There's been a lot of fighting here in recent months and the old hands are glad to have reinforcements. No one's told us what we're going to be doing yet, but I'm confident that we'll be well prepared for whatever it is.

I met another New Yorker here in the camp. He lives near us, on 78th, close to the river. His name is Gervasio Bartali. His mom and dad run a delicatessen at number 468.

"Hey, I know where that is," said Linus. "I almost go past it on the way to Castelli's."

"Be quiet!" shouted Willy. Max elbowed Linus and glared at him. Their father looked around the table and waited.

> It feels good to have someone from home around being so far away, even though I don't really know him. We talk about places in New York that we both know and about our families. And he told me about something that's been bugging him for weeks. It has to do with his mom. His family has this strange tradition of giving their mom a fright on her birthday. They say it's good for her health, something to do with her circulation. The bigger the fright, the better, since they want to make sure she stays healthy for the coming year. So on her birthday, Gervasio always used to hide a spider (or two) somewhere in the house. In the sugar bowl, the cash drawer, a box of matches in the kitchen. He's only got one brother, who's gone off to war, too, so he's worried the tradition won't be continued this year… But when he heard that I have four brothers, he asked if one of you might be able to help. It sounds like the perfect job for you, Linus. And the great thing is that his mom thinks she doesn't need to be on her guard this year! Here's the plan: every Wednesday and Sunday evening, his mom puts out the box for the milkman. Not a homemade one like ours, but a proper one, made of metal, that you can use to keep things cold. You can't see it from the street—they keep it in a little alcove beside the door. The milkman comes at around six o'clock the next morning and leaves two bottles of milk in the box. His mom brings in the milk at seven. That means, Linus, that on Monday, December 6, you have one hour to add a couple of live spiders to the box. And a card from

Gervasio, which I'm sending with this letter. He says hi and thanks a lot. And so will his mom, once she's recovered from the shock!

It's hard to imagine that life is just going on as usual for all of you. How are things at the paper, Simon? Does old Mercier still have a really short fuse? And is Mrs. Ling's coffee in the canteen still like muddy water? Never thought I'd long to hold a cup of that slop in my hands! What they call coffee here is only like the real thing because it's hot, and sometimes it's not even that. Hi, Max, are you keeping Willy in line? Or are the two of you letting Sis boss you around? Linus, do you know we get piles of new comics delivered here? Everyone pounces on them and devours the latest stories. Have you seen the picture on the cover of the most recent one? If only we had motorbikes like that for real...

I'm thinking of you all and missing you, or at least I am whenever I have enough time! A big kiss for Mom and for Sis.

Ciao!

Your Alberto

Their father folded up the letter. He took a smaller envelope out of the big one and put it down flat on the table. Everyone crowded around. *Signora Bartali*, it said in small spiky letters.

"Hands off! All of you, hands off!" Their mother picked up the envelope and held it up in the air, away from all the grubby little fingers. She had shaken her head in disbelief when their father had read out the part about Gervasio's mother, but now she was smiling.

"I'll keep it for you," she said, winking at Linus. She slipped it into the drawer of the sideboard with the important papers. With the other letters from Albie.

17

Linus couldn't wait to tell Liam about his mission. He'd be sure to want to help when he heard about it. Maybe the two of them could meet up tomorrow after he had made his deliveries and go on a scouting expedition to Bartali's. Linus didn't want to leave anything to chance. Nothing could be allowed to go wrong on December 6th.

But when he got to school the next morning, Liam wasn't in the usual place. And he couldn't find him anywhere that afternoon after school either. They usually waited for each other and walked part of the way home together, but lately Liam hardly seemed to have time for anything. When Linus had gone by on Saturday so that they could go and buy the latest *Action Comics* together, Liam hadn't even come outside. He'd just shouted down from the window that he had to help his father. And that was strange because, unlike Linus, Liam hardly ever had to help out at home.

Linus didn't have time to dawdle since he had deliveries to make, so he'd just have to make his first scouting expedition alone. If he had time after, he would drop by Liam's for a little while.

He kept Castelli's until the end of his round, and once he'd made his delivery to the restaurant he walked along 78th Street in the direction of the East River. He could read the sign from the other side of the street: BARTALI'S DELICATESSEN. It was busy in the store. A short, stout man stood behind the counter. Linus watched as the man climbed a ladder to fetch something from a high shelf. There were so many customers going in and out of the store that Linus was confident he wouldn't be noticed. He parked his cart behind a newspaper stand and crossed the street.

When he got close to the sign, he could see that the capital letters B and D were each made up of a string of painted sausages. As he walked past the window, doing his best not to be noticed, a woman came out from the back of the store. She was wearing an apron like his mother's over her dress, with a big pocket in the middle. That was all he'd glimpsed by the time he'd passed the window.

He went on for a while before turning around. When he got back to the window, the woman was standing behind the counter beside the man. She was as short as he and almost as round. The man had put one arm around her shoulders and was saying something to a customer, waving his other hand in the air. The people in the store were laughing. The woman laughed with them, a little shyly, and put her hands in the pocket over her belly. She had a funny smile, and Linus couldn't help smiling back. As he did so, he realized that he had stopped in front of the window again. Just as he was about to leave, he noticed the pennant in the bottom left corner of the window. It wasn't so obvious that it seemed like showing off, but it was still perfectly visible. Two blue stars! Linus felt his heart beating faster.

This has to work out, thought Linus as he crossed back over the street. He looked one more time at the blue stars. Doing a favor for a soldier was also a way of helping out in the war. Maybe not the same as stopping a U-boat all by himself... but he still wanted his mission to succeed. Mrs. Bartali's health was at stake. And he wanted Albie to be proud of him.

He hurried down the street. He still had enough time to swing by Liam's before dinner. *And who knows? Maybe Rosie will be at home*, thought Linus as he turned the corner of Liam's block. And she could hear his story, too...

Linus stopped. MacKenna was standing at Liam's front door, leaning comfortably with one arm on the doorframe. *He must be chatting with Rosie*, Linus thought as he started walking again, though more slowly than before. MacKenna would be sure to make one of his nasty remarks when Linus told them about his mission. He really wasn't in the mood for that... but he wanted to tell Liam his news.

He stopped again. It wasn't Rosie that MacKenna was talking to—it was Liam! He was laughing at something that MacKenna had said, but then he looked over MacKenna's shoulder, straight at Linus. Liam's smile vanished immediately and was replaced by a strange expression—as though he'd been caught out.

MacKenna turned his head to see what Liam was looking at. When he saw Linus, a lopsided grin spread across his face. Then he shrugged and looked back at Liam.

Linus turned around and headed back up the block. "Linus!" Liam shouted. Linus started walking faster. *He'll follow me*, he thought. *And he'll tell me I've got it all wrong. There's no way Liam is going to become pals with someone like Georgie MacKenna.*

But when Liam still hadn't caught up with him by the time he reached the corner, Linus looked back and saw that he was still standing at the door with MacKenna. He was looking directly at Linus, but he didn't do anything. He didn't even shout for him to wait. Nothing at all.

So that was why Liam was so busy all the time! Because he was suddenly best buddies with MacKenna. Linus stomped around the corner. It probably made him feel special that an older boy was hanging out with him.

Well, if that was what he wanted, fine. Linus shrugged and started walking faster. If Liam would rather hang out with MacKenna, then he could just go ahead and do that. Linus could manage perfectly well without him.

18

The very best place for catching spiders was out in the yard, in the dark corner by the potato storage bin. The spiders in there were so big that they almost scared even Linus. On Sunday afternoon, as part of his careful preparations for the next day, he had caught two and put them in a jam jar with holes in the lid.

On Monday morning, his father woke him before leaving for the market. Still groggy, Linus went downstairs and found that his mother was already up, too. She gave him the envelope and unlocked the front door for him.

"Come straight back," she told him. Outside, the cold air woke him up immediately. From the corner, he quickly looked back and saw his mother still standing there. He raised his hand, but didn't wait to see if she waved back.

He held the jam jar under his jacket. The envelope with the card was tucked safely into his belt. At a brisk pace, it was twelve minutes from his house to Bartali's.

It was still dark out and the wind was icy cold. It wasn't even half past six by the time he reached his destination. At the corner, he passed the milkman, who was whistling a happy tune. He gave Linus a wink. It almost seemed like a sign: the coast is clear. At that moment, Linus couldn't help thinking about Liam. It would have been so much fun for the two of them… *But I can't think about that now*, thought Linus. Then he took a deep breath and looked at the store on the other side of the street.

"Need a hand?" Mister Superspeed is hovering in the air just above Linus, his thumbs hooked into his red belt. The color makes a nice contrast with his yellow suit. "Here, let me take the jar."

"No!" he shouts. His voice echoes through the empty street. He looks around, alarmed, but there's no one in sight. The milkman has disappeared around the corner.

"Really. I can do it quick as a flash. No one will see me." Mister Superspeed circles around him, trying to take the jam jar from him.

"I'll do it myself." Linus is spinning around in circles too now, trying to keep the jam jar away from Mister Superspeed. "It's my mission." He won't let anyone take it away from him. "Anyway, don't you have other jobs to do?" Even his whispering sounds loud in the quiet street. "Putting U-boats out of action? Moving wounded soldiers out of the firing line? Dealing with bombs?"

"I do that all day," says Mister Superspeed. "Can't I have a bit of fun for once?" He starts circling in the opposite direction, taking Linus by surprise.

"You're messing up my plan!" growls Linus. Mister Superspeed is really starting to get on his nerves. "What if someone sees me?"

"Oh, I see." Mister Superspeed sounds indignant. "I'm only supposed to do the dirty work."

"Dirty work? Linus is so furious that he forgets to whisper. "We're talking about soldiers' lives!"

"Okay, okay, I'm going." Mister Superspeed puts his hands up, as though he's surrendering. "I was only joking." But he's not smiling.

Linus hears footsteps behind him. Startled, he looks around.

A man was walking toward him, his hat pulled down over his eyes to protect them from the wind. Linus held his breath and waited. He didn't let himself breathe again until the man had passed. When he looked back over his shoulder, Mister Superspeed had gone.

He held the jar tightly as he crossed the street. It was still dark inside Bartali's. By the light of a lamppost, he soon spotted the metal milk box. He knelt down, put the jam jar on the sidewalk and lifted the lid. Two bottles of milk. Everything was going fine so far.

Linus looked around. He saw two pedestrians crossing the street in the distance, but they were still far enough away. He pulled the envelope out of his belt and slipped it behind the bottles.

Carefully, he unscrewed the jam jar. The spiders were sitting there, perfectly still. They were two absolute beauties. He put his hand into the jar and fished them out. They tickled his palm as they tried to escape. A shiver ran down his spine. He put the hand with the spiders into the milk box and held down the lid as well as he could with the other. It was really cold inside the box. Much colder than it was outside. Would the spiders feel the cold? No, he mustn't hesitate now! Any longer and he would start to feel sorry for them.

He opened up his hand and felt the spiders crawl down into the box. Then he snatched back his hand and dropped the lid.

Mission accomplished, he stood up and ran across the street. There was a dark doorway facing the deli from where he'd have a good view of the store. But it was too cold to stand still for long. To warm himself up, he started walking back and forth along the street. It was just beginning to drizzle.

As he was wondering whether he should head home, a light flickered on in the back of the store. He saw a shadow moving through the delicatessen. The door opened and a small round silhouette came into view. He couldn't make out whether it was Mrs. Bartali or Mr. Bartali. The person stooped down to pick up the box. The door closed again, and about ten seconds later the light went out.

Without really knowing what he was waiting for, Linus stood looking through the dark shop window for a short while after. Perhaps he'd been hoping to hear a scream... but nothing happened.

Slowly, he walked away. He didn't start running until he had turned the corner. He had done it! Albie would be so proud of him. Linus felt happy as he ran through the dark streets. He was even starting to feel warm again.

So far, so good. But he'd have to wait for the next letter from Europe to find out if it had been a real success.

19

Nothing was going to spoil Linus's good mood. Not the rain, which was pouring down now, and definitely not Liam. Linus had spotted him crossing the street after school, with his shoulders hunched up against the rain. They hadn't spoken a word since he had stormed off from Liam's house last week. And now, whenever he caught sight of Liam, he turned his back on him.

With his cap pulled down over his brow, Linus tried to steer the cart around the puddles. There was a huge pile of furniture out on the sidewalk on 76th Street. To get past, Linus had to pull his cart down into the street for a short way. As he gently bumped the cart back up onto the sidewalk, he spotted something familiar out of the corner of his eye. That coat rack on the pile of furniture… the strange one with the antlers. It was just like the one in Mrs. De Winter's hallway. Linus stopped and pushed up his cap.

That was when he noticed that Mrs. De Winter's door was open. Two men were walking in and out, adding more and more things to the pile. He could see other things that he recognized.

"Where's that van got to?" one man called from the hallway. The other man put down a chair, shrugged his shoulders and pointed at the traffic, which was crawling forward slowly in the pouring rain.

Linus hadn't delivered anything to Mrs. De Winter's since Halloween. Suddenly he felt really mean for not having thought about her at all. And now all of her things were lying out on the sidewalk for everyone to see, and no one cared that they were getting wet. The men walked around, whistling. If Mrs. De Winter could see what was going on, she'd take charge right away. Short as she was, she could still boss those big men around with her loud voice. The thought made Linus grin. Then he tugged his cap back down and went on his way.

By the time he arrived at Mr. Orange's building, he was soaked through. But he brightened up when he entered the building and could already hear Mr. Orange's music wafting down from upstairs.

"It's a drowned rat!" Mr. Orange shouted down when he saw Linus. "You're going to get a cold, young man."

Linus put down the crate beside the kitchen door and shook the drops of water from his cap. Suddenly, he started to shiver. Now that he was out of the rain, he realized just how cold he was.

"Ah, you poor thing. Give me your wet jacket. We need to get you warmed up before I send you back out into the streets." Holding out the dripping jacket in front of him, Mr. Orange walked through the kitchen. Linus followed.

It was bright and warm in the studio. Mr. Orange hung Linus's jacket by the radiator and pulled up a stool for him. "I was just making a pot of tea," he said as he headed back into the kitchen.

Linus sat down by the radiator and felt the warmth on his back. Music filled the room. A piano played short, fast notes and a trumpet tootled away as though it was trying to confuse the piano. As Linus's eyes wandered around the room, his feet automatically started tapping along with the rhythm. The rain was pounding down so hard on the windowpanes that it sounded as though it was trying to join in.

There were a lot of new colored shapes on the walls. A row of brushes lay side by side on the high window seat. Their bristly heads all extended exactly the same distance over the edge, as though they were peering down. A palette with a few blobs of paint lay beside them. In the warmth of the room, the smell of paint was even stronger than usual.

The music had just finished when Mr. Orange came back with the tea. He handed Linus a cup and walked over to the record player.

"A dance hall for painting in…" he said as he turned over the record, "can also be a studio for dancing in." He held up one finger and waited for the music to begin again.

"This is the best dance music ever! Let me show you how to do it." He turned the music up and started clapping his hands. This tune was even faster than the one before. With both hands around the warm cup, Linus watched Mr. Orange intently as he danced. His thin body remained almost completely still. Only his feet and lower arms moved. He held his arms out at an angle and repeatedly flicked them to the side, very fast and very stiff, to the beat of the music. He held his head at a slight tilt, while his feet made little hops all the way to the wall behind him.

"You should try it!" He beckoned to Linus as he came hopping back. "It'll cheer you up, and your pants will dry more quickly, too."

Linus hesitated. He'd sometimes waltzed around the living room at home with Albie to help him practice for his dancing class. But that music had been easy. It was the kind of tune that stayed in your head even after the music had stopped.

"You see? Horizontal and vertical! All at the same time. It's the new way to dance," said Mr. Orange, hopping up and down the studio like a big bird. But the expression on his face was perfectly serious.

Linus could feel himself starting to smile. He quickly stood up and started to move with the music, trying to join in without thinking too much about it.

"Too much swing!" Mr. Orange shouted above the music. "Keep those hips still!"

Linus tried it again. How was it possible to move the legs without moving the hips at the same time? This new way of dancing wasn't as easy as it looked.

"Too much hip!" sang Mr. Orange as he danced off again with his precise hops. He was panting a little now, and he kept coughing. Linus put his hands on his hips to keep them still, but they wouldn't stop swaying very slightly all by themselves. When the music ended, he dropped down onto the window seat. Mr. Orange continued his hop all the way over to the window, even without the music.

They sat together, catching their breath. The only sounds were the *shh-click-shh-click* of the needle on the record and the rain. Linus felt warm again.

"Boogie-woogie is the perfect city music, don't you think?" Mr. Orange took off his glasses and wiped his forehead with the back of his hand. Sitting that close to him, Linus could really see the dark circles under his eyes.

"If you listen carefully, you can hear the hustle and bustle. Everything is changing all the time. There's one rhythm, and then another cuts through it, but it all still fits together. That's the rhythm of New York." Mr. Orange's eyes were gleaming.

"Far and near, quick and slow, light and dark… In the city, it's all there at the same time. That's what I try to show in my work." He seemed to be talking to himself, his eyes focused on the easel at the far end of the room. There was a large square canvas on the easel that faced the wall, so all Linus could see was the back of it. One of its corners pointed upward, turning the square into a diamond. It was the only painting in the whole room.

"In this painting, I'm almost there… I've finally managed to get boogie-woogie into it." He clapped his hands and stood up. "When it's finished I'll show it to you, and then you'll see what I mean." He picked up Linus's jacket, checked to see if it was dry, and then held it up for Linus to put on. Linus slipped his arms into the sleeves. The jacket felt warm and cozy now.

It was still raining outside. Linus looked up. The rain made the stone of the building look even darker. From the street, there was no sign of the bright room that lay concealed behind that dull, gray façade, right in the middle of the busy city. It reminded Linus of Sis's music box. On the outside, it didn't look like anything special, but once it was opened there was an unexpected world inside.

Linus pulled down his cap and began his walk home. *In a way*, he thought, *that white room is now inside my head as well.*

It felt as though that place up there belonged to him, too. Like a box that he could open whenever he wanted.

Snatches of the music he had heard floated in and out of his head. He whistled a few notes until he couldn't remember what came next. Then, as other notes came to him, he hummed a few more.

Linus walked through the crowds of people in the rush-hour bustle. Now and then he danced a few steps through the rain to the music in his head. His hips swayed along, all by themselves.

20

It's strange, thought Linus, *how easy it is to get used to waiting.* They'd gotten used to the mailman walking past the store every day with a friendly wave, but no mail. Even their neighbor Mrs. Hensen had stopped coming by every single day. And when she did come into the store, his mother answered her questions as well as she could, all the while tugging at her fingers.

So Linus and his mother were both a little surprised when, instead of walking by, the mailman opened the store door one rainy afternoon, tipped his wet hat, and placed an envelope on the counter. Linus had just finished packing his cart. He walked over to the counter and found himself looking at Albie's familiar, neat handwriting.

His mother dabbed away the drops of rain on the envelope with a corner of her apron and dropped it into her pocket with a sigh. Even though it would be a long wait, Linus knew there was no chance of the envelope being opened until they were all gathered around the table at dinnertime. The idea of having to wait for the next few hours almost seemed worse than all of the weeks of waiting that had gone before. So Linus was happy that he had his delivery round to keep him busy.

Mrs. Hensen turned up just as Linus was taking the cart outside. His mother caught his eye and winked at him. The sparkle was back in her eyes. Today she could deal with a thousand nosy neighbors, if she had to.

Their father insisted that everyone's plate had to be empty before he would read out the letter. But Willy pushed his spinach around for so long that even their mother couldn't stand it any longer and—"Just this once!"—snatched his plate away. Everyone sat in perfect silence as their father opened the letter. He looked around the table before starting to read.

Dear Mom and Dad, dear Sis and brothers,
   Mom wrote that Dad reads out my letters with everyone sitting around the table. That sounds like fun. I'd love to be there with you.

Their father looked around again and smiled.

But part of this letter…

Their father stopped reading. His eyes flew over the lines.
   "Keep going!" Max was rocking on his chair.
   "Abbie! Abbie! Abbie!" Sis banged her two little fists on the table.
   Linus held his breath. He saw their father turn over the piece of paper, read it, and then turn it over again. Then he glanced at their mother before clearing his throat and starting again.

Dear Mom and Dad, dear Sis and brothers,

Mom wrote that Dad reads out my letters with everyone sitting around the table. That sounds like fun. I'd love to be there with you.

How are you all doing? I'm sorry I didn't write sooner. It can sometimes take a while for a soldier to find a bit of time and space to write a letter in the middle of all this commotion. Holding a pen feels strange now that my fingers are used to doing completely different work: cleaning my gun or making a dugout.

It's pretty cold and bleak up here in the mountains, and it rains almost constantly. I can hardly believe I ever complained about my bed at home. After a few nights in a dugout (which we had to dig ourselves), I'd kill for my own bed. But if you're tired enough, you can learn to sleep anywhere. Tonight, though, I'm in an army tent. The wind's tugging at the canvas and the whole thing's flapping around, but in a strange way it's almost cozy. Finally a chance to rest and to write you a letter. And hopefully to warm up my feet!

I miss you all so much, and I even miss the city—isn't that crazy? After all I've said about New York being too busy and stinking of automobiles, what I wouldn't give to be able to walk down our street right now, just for a moment, and look in through the store window. Even though there's no one there, of course, because you're all sitting upstairs with my letter...

Lots of love to everyone,
Your Albie

"Abbie! Abbie!" Sis clapped her hands. Linus looked up at his father with a puzzled expression.

"Didn't he say anything about Gervasio's mom?"

His father coughed. Then he folded the letter and put it back in the envelope.

"He didn't say if it worked? If I gave his mom a fright?" Linus watched the envelope disappearing into his father's jacket pocket. "He can't have just forgotten about it!"

His father exchanged glances with his mother. Then he stood up to go downstairs and make the list for the market tomorrow, as he always did.

"Albie has more important things on his mind. Got that, you dope?" Simon stood up and gave Linus's shoulder a whack. Linus hardly noticed. His eyes were fixed on his father's back, which was disappearing into the hallway and down the stairs.

"Just leave it, Linus." His mother gently laid her hand on his shoulder.

"But—"

"Think about the little ones." Her hand became heavier. Linus looked around the table. Three pairs of eyes were staring at him. Max and Willy looked curious, and Sis looked worried. Her bottom lip was trembling as if she might start to cry at any moment.

Linus stood up. He suddenly felt as though he couldn't breathe. He needed to get some air. He ran out of the room, grabbed his jacket, and raced down the stairs and through the store. The front door was open. His father was taking out a pile of empty crates to the van. Without saying a word, Linus shot past him and into the street. He thought he heard his father shouting something after him but he wasn't sure. And right now, he really didn't care.

21

The wind was vicious, and Linus had forgotten his gloves at home. He shoved his hands deep into his pockets. The cold bit at his lungs. And the wind blasted into his face, as if it was doing its best to stop him. *If you want a fight, you've got it!* thought Linus. He was in the mood for a fight, and battling the wind would do just fine.

He hunched up and leaned forward. He had to run. Fast. Down the street, around the corner, and straight on he went, without thinking, farther and farther in one direction, trying to outrun himself and his thoughts, which kept spinning around one point: Albie. He didn't come to a stop until he felt like his lungs were about to burst and he could barely catch a single breath. He stood there panting, leaning forward with his hands on his knees.

It took him a while to realize that he was standing on the corner of the block where Liam lived. For a split second, he wished that he could go and tell Liam about Albie, about the letter…but he wasn't ready to stop being mad at him yet.

And anyway, what could Liam have said? That he'd been stupid enough to take a silly joke seriously? That he had waited and waited for a message from his brother, but Albie had already forgotten about the whole thing?

Linus straightened up and started to run again.

"Wait for me!"

He doesn't need to look around to know that Mister Superspeed is behind him. He doesn't care. He keeps on running. Then he's out of breath again, but it feels good. It makes his head feel light and giddy.

"Hey, don't let it worry you!" Mister Superspeed still hasn't caught up with him. "Better luck next time."

"Leave me alone!" He sprints forward, moving faster and faster. The cold air hurts his lungs and stings his throat, but still he runs, flying down the street. A car honks. He barely notices. He runs until he's so tired that he almost trips and finally has to slow down, his heart pounding away like crazy.

Finally, Mister Superspeed catches up with him.

"Since when does a superhero struggle to keep up with an ordinary boy?" he says as soon as he can speak again.

"Not an ordinary boy. An angry boy." Mister Superspeed is panting just as much as Linus. "You know, I think angry boys have superpowers." He leans on a lamppost. "And okay, maybe I'm a little off my game. Even superheroes have a bad day sometimes."

"Sure you're not working too hard? Mending your costume must be exhausting." He can hear how mean his words sound, but he doesn't care

"My uniform," says Mister Superspeed, correcting him. "And in case you've forgotten—there's a war on."

"What did you mean by 'Better luck next time'?"

"Just... that it might have been easier if you'd let me help with your first mission." Mister Superspeed puts his hand on Linus's shoulder and gives him a strange look. It makes Linus uncomfortable, even though he isn't exactly sure what the look means. "Albie must have asked you to do it because he knew I'd be able to help."

"Mission? That stupid joke, you mean." He shakes Mister Superspeed's hand from his shoulder and starts walking. "Anyway, do you think you could have done it better? Using superspiders or something?"

There's no answer, so he looks around. Mister Superspeed is sitting on a stoop, catching his breath, his elbows on his knees. He still has that strange look in his eyes.

Linus shrugs impatiently and keeps on going.

It wasn't until he had turned the corner that Linus found the right word for the strange expression on Mister Superspeed's face. It was pity. Mister Superspeed looked as though he felt sorry for Linus.

Why? Because his brother had forgotten about him? Linus shook his head. The longer he thought about it, the harder it was to believe that. Albie would never forget him. There was something else going on. He thought about his father, who had looked at him in the same way. Was that pity too? His father had paused in the middle of a sentence. *But part of this letter...*

Linus stopped short. What if he'd gotten it all wrong? What if the joke had gotten out of hand? Maybe the spiders Linus had picked were too scary and Gervasio's mother had had such a fright that he'd spoiled her whole birthday. Maybe Albie had asked his parents not to tell Linus about it. "*But part of this letter isn't meant for Linus...*"

Was that what Mister Superspeed had meant? That if Linus had let him help, it wouldn't have gotten out of hand? He turned and ran back to the corner, but the stoop was empty. Mister Superspeed was nowhere to be seen.

22

Linus decided he would ask his mother about the letter when she was on her own in the store the next day. It was usually easier to get secrets out of her than his father. But when he came home after making his deliveries that afternoon, the store was busy.

"Max took the little ones out to play," she said as Linus walked out to the back. "Will you start peeling the potatoes?" She sounded tired. The sparkle that had been in her eyes yesterday was gone.

Linus put away the cart and went upstairs. His father's quiet snoring was the only sound in the house. He carried the potatoes, which were piled up on an old newspaper, into the front room. Then he fetched a pan of water and sat down at the table.

The house wasn't this quiet very often. He dropped the first potato into the water with a splash. The silence made it even more difficult not to think about the letter. He picked up the next potato.

His father's jacket was hanging on the back of the chair opposite him. Linus's eyes kept straying to it, but he was determined to keep on peeling the potatoes.

All the same, his eyes did their own thing, sliding from the tip of the knife to the inside pocket of the jacket. If he leaned a little to one side, he could just make out the edge of the envelope sticking out…

"Ow!" The knife sliced into his finger. He dropped the knife and put his finger into his mouth. Now that he had to wait for the bleeding to stop, he had plenty of time to stare at the little bit of white sticking out from the inside pocket. He wasn't supposed to be looking at it at all. He was supposed to be peeling the potatoes. He would just have to ask about the letter later, when the little ones were in bed.

With his finger still in his mouth, he stood up. He walked around the table and leaned over the jacket. His other hand touched the white edge of the envelope. Then, it was in his hand.

Listening carefully to his father's snoring, he slid the letter out of the envelope. His hands shook as his eyes ran over the words.

Dear Mom and Dad, dear Sis and brothers,
 Mom wrote that Dad reads out my letters with everyone sitting around the table. That sounds like fun. I'd love to be there with you. (But part of this letter isn't meant for reading out loud. I've put it in brackets. That section's just for you and Mom.)
 How are you all doing? I'm sorry I didn't write sooner…

I should stop now, thought Linus. *Stop and fold up the letter and put it back into the envelope and into the pocket.* But his hands wouldn't listen and his eyes raced on, over the part he already knew, until he came to a bracket.

Finally a chance to rest and to write you a letter. And hopefully to warm up my feet! (I don't know what's wrong with them, but they're itching terribly. It's like the cold's eating away at them. And it seems to be getting worse and worse. They always warn you here that you need to keep your feet dry. But how can you have dry feet when you're out in the rain all day and night?

Linus's eyes were unstoppable. They rolled on and on, like a tank.

How could I ever have thought we were well prepared? What a joke. Shows how much I know! How can anyone prepare for a war? We're just back from a battle—and it was a disaster. Lots of men were wounded or killed. Including Gervasio, the boy from New York I told you about. He was hit by a grenade. They took him to a field hospital, but he didn't make it. Like so many other men. It's a terrible thing to say, but you get used to it so quickly. But with someone as close as Gervasio, a guy I spent a lot of time with… it hits you hard. Maybe I shouldn't be telling you this. I know Mom's already so worried and so are you. But it's a relief to be able to tell someone about it. All the men around me have their own horror stories, so we try not to spend too much time talking to each other about them.

I know I sound bitter, but I'm trying to keep in mind what we're doing it all for. It's just that this war keeps throwing poison at us…)

I miss you all so much, and I even miss the city—isn't that crazy?

Linus stared at the paper. How could Albie's small, neat handwriting describe such awful things? He felt sick. Like he'd sneaked too many spoonfuls of sugar from the sugar bowl.

Too much sugar? Too much poison.

Too many words.

His hands were shaking. He could hear a child crying out on the street. Was it Sis?

He folded the letter and tried to put it back into the envelope, but his fingers felt clumsy. Some of the blood from his cut finger ended up on the envelope. He tried to wipe it off but only made the mark bigger. He heard Sis and Max downstairs below the window, and he heard the bell ring in the store. Finally he got the letter back into its envelope, and he quickly tucked it back inside his father's pocket. By the time Max and the little ones had stomped up the stairs, he was back in his chair. He picked up a potato and stared at it, feeling a little dizzy.

Willy and Sis ran squabbling into the bedroom where their father was napping.

Max came into the living room and sat down opposite him, on the chair with the jacket, without saying a word. He rested his head on the table and groaned. Linus knew just how infuriating the little ones could be. Then their father came in from the bedroom, holding hands with Willy and Sis, their fight now over. His eyes were still heavy with sleep.

"What's up with you?" he said to Linus, who was still staring at the potato in his hand. "You look pale."

"I cut my finger," Linus said quickly. He held up his hand.

His father came over to take a look. "Is that why you're shaking? You look like you've seen a ghost."

"I'm fine now." Linus pulled his hand away. Then the fight between Sis and Willy flared up again, and his father's attention turned elsewhere. Linus took a deep breath, picked up the knife, and went back to the potatoes.

23

"What's going on?" Linus mumbled drowsily. He tried to open his eyes. He'd been tossing and turning for hours, and now that he was finally starting to fall asleep someone was shaking his bed.

"How else do you expect me to get up to my bunk?" said a grumpy voice. "I can't fly, you know."

Oh, it's just Simon... Linus rolled over onto his other side.

But no, it's not Simon at all. It's a soldier climbing up a ladder. He has attached a brush to the point of his bayonet and is daubing gray paint onto a wall. "Everything between brackets has to go!" *he shouts. Another soldier appears, his brush at the ready, forcing Linus back. From a distance, he can see that the entire wall is covered with colored shapes. Hundreds of soldiers are attacking it with their brushes. From where he is, they look like tiny tin soldiers.*

Mister Superspeed tiptoes over from behind. He has taken off his blue boots and carries one in each hand. Little sputtering sounds come from the soles as though they are protesting, but there's no steam. "My feet are so itchy," *he says.* "And it seems to be getting worse and worse."

"Do something," Linus shouts. "They're painting over the colors! Can't you do anything to help?"

Wincing, Mister Superspeed lifts up one foot and gives it a careful pinch. "This itch is driving me crazy."

"Did you even hear what I said?" Linus yells, shaking him. "These are the colors of the future! And speaking of helping, why didn't you save that soldier?"

"There are so many of them. I can't keep up."

"He was Albie's friend!"

"Everyone is somebody's friend," says Mister Superspeed. "You can't expect me to take that into account." Tiny soldiers gather around him. They don't even reach as far as his ankles, but they hook onto his costume and start climbing up his legs. The bright yellow disappears under the paint, as quick as lightning. Linus tries to pluck the soldiers off him, but for every two he gets, there seem to be four new ones.

"There are too many of them." Mister Superspeed flaps his hands at the soldiers as though they're pesky little flies. They've already reached his red belt. Now Linus's feet are starting to itch too. Little soldiers are climbing all over them, heading for his calves. They stab at the back of his knees, and he yells and hits and kicks to shake them off. "Keep still! How am I supposed to paint like this?"

As he thrashed about, Linus's foot hit something hard and he shot up, his heart pounding.

"Keep still!" growled Simon. "How am I supposed to sleep like this?"

Throwing back his covers, Linus got up and sat on the edge of his bed. Above him, Simon muttered something and then started snoring quietly again.

All alone in the dark, with only the words from the letter to keep him company, Linus felt trapped. Maybe he could go and sit in the living room for a while with the light on. Then he'd soon feel better. He groped around in the dark for his sweater and socks and quietly stood up.

He could hear the soft murmur of voices coming from the living room. Were his parents still awake? He tiptoed closer and rested his forehead against the door so that he could hear their familiar voices. So that he could begin to calm down.

"I'm not coming with you." His mother's voice was soft.

Silence.

"I can't go. I just can't." Linus could barely make out her words.

"But it's their *son*." His father's voice went up high, as if surprised by what she had said.

"I don't know these people. I've never even met them."

"He was our son's friend."

Silence.

"What if it were the other way around?"

A loud bang. Linus jumped.

"Don't you dare, Bert." The word "dare" was accompanied by another bang, as his mother slapped the table again. "Don't you dare even think that thought. Not in this house. Not about our Albie."

Linus froze on the spot. The silence that followed was longer than the previous one. He started to shiver. He needed to get back into bed. He turned around.

He heard someone push back a chair.

"Then I'll go on my own." His father's voice was calm.

Linus dashed across the hallway and dived into his bed as the living room door opened. With the covers pulled up to his chin, he listened to his father's footsteps on the stairs. He was still shivering long after he heard the bell jangle on the door downstairs. He just couldn't get warm, no matter how much he tossed from side to side.

With his eyes wide open, he listened to the sounds his mother made as she went to bed. When everything was quiet, he slipped out of bed and walked to his parents' room. He felt his way to their bed in the darkness and stood there, suddenly uncertain. As a little boy, he often used to climb into bed with his mother when the sounds of his father going to the market woke him up. Now it was only the little ones who did that.

"Linus." He heard her push back the covers. How did she know he was there in the dark?

Once he was in the big bed, he soon warmed up. His mother didn't say anything, but he knew she was awake. He did his best to stay awake with her, but his body felt heavier and heavier and he soon drifted off to sleep.

24

"Watch where you're going!"

Linus jumped. A lady in a fashionable suit gave him an irritated look before turning around, her heels angrily tapping their way through the crowd.

It was not the first time that afternoon that he'd almost bumped into somebody because his mind was on the letter and not on his cart. Albie's words haunted him all the way along his route. Very slowly, he was beginning to realize just how stupid he'd been. The world was at war, and he was worried about playing tricks with spiders. Something terrible had happened in Italy—and all he'd been able to think about was himself. He didn't have a clue! But that was all going to change, starting now. He felt more determined than ever as he pulled the cart after him.

When he got home he saw the blue star right away. It was in the store window, in the bottom left corner. Linus pulled the cart through to the back. Then he picked up an old newspaper from the pile and walked back into the store.

"What's that doing there?" he asked when his mother had finished serving her customer. He pointed at the window.

"I changed my mind." His mother had her back to him, but she knew what he meant without having to look. She closed the cash drawer and made a note in the order book. Then she turned around.

"Everyone should know that Albie is risking his life for their freedom." She looked at him calmly.

The bell jangled.

Linus picked up a ball of string from the counter, cut two long pieces, and wound them around his hand. With the newspaper under his arm, he headed upstairs. It was crazy—only a few days ago he'd have been so proud of that star. He'd have thought it was brave and exciting. But now it just reminded him of the letter and of the other blue stars, the ones in Bartali's window.

He spread out a few sheets of newspaper on the floor. Then he knelt down and pulled out the nearest pile of *Action Comics* from beneath the bed. He lifted the pile onto a sheet of newspaper, folded the newspaper around the comics, and took some string, tying it tight around the package. He spread out the rest of the sheets of newspaper and pulled out the other pile of comics. He wrapped the newspaper around them and was about to pick up the other piece of string, but changed his mind. Instead, he reached under the bed for the notebooks and lifted the stack onto his lap. The notebook on the top of the pile fell open to a drawing of Mister Superspeed blocking a hail of grenades and bullets with his arms and shielding a soldier.

"*What are you doing?*" Mister Superspeed bats a bullet away with his fist. He's watching Linus out of the corner of his eye.

"*I'm tidying up. I should have done it a long time ago.*"

"Tidying up? Are you trying to get rid of me?" Mister Superspeed makes it sound like a joke, but he can tell Mister Superspeed's a bit worried.

He picks up the piece of string.

"You can't be serious!" Mister Superspeed almost misses a grenade. "But why? Just because I have the occasional bad day?"

He shakes his head. "That's not what it's about."

"But I'm doing my best! It's not always easy, not even for a superhero. Anyway, everything's going fine now. Here, look." He catches a grenade with one hand and throws it up into the sky. He does a pirouette before catching it with his other hand and throwing it far into the distance. "You see?" He taps his helmet. "I'm shipshape again!"

Linus watches his tricks in silence. How did he ever think that Mister Superspeed could help? He'd just been dreaming with his eyes wide open. All that time he'd been hiding from the real world, safe behind Mister Superspeed's broad back.

But Mister Superspeed isn't helping at all.

Linus shrugs and turns the page.

"I'm doing the best I can!" Mister Superspeed calls out from the next page. He's holding up a burning airplane, keeping it in the air. "See, I really am helping!"

No, not really, thinks Linus. Not in the real world.

"Wait!" shouts Mister Superspeed. The steam from his boots hisses noisily, like a cornered cat. "We've always been such good friends, the three of us... You, me... and Albie..."

"That's what I thought too," Linus says with a frown. "But you're the one who sent him off to war."

"Excuse me?" Mister Superspeed forgets about the plane. It goes into a dive, its engine roaring. "If I remember correctly, your brother volunteered."

"Yes, because you made it seem like it's easy to win a war! Like it's no big deal, like you can beat the whole lousy bunch of them with one hand tied behind your back. You make war seem exciting, like an adventure, like something out of a comic. But it's not like that. That's all just imaginary."

"Since when has there been anything wrong with imagining things?" asks Mister Superspeed. He sounds astonished. But he has the plane under control again and is pointing it up into the sky.

"I'm not saying there's anything wrong with it…" Linus looks uneasily at the string in his hands. "It's just that Simon's right. I'm getting too big for make-believe."

"So you're now listening to that grouchy brother of yours? As if he knows anything about the imagination! Look at me!" Mister Superspeed slaps his broad chest. "I'm not too old to imagine things, am I?"

"Imagination's not going to win any wars." Linus pauses, picking at a corner of the newspaper. "Imagination's not going to help you protect Albie. You can't promise me he'll be safe."

"Of course he will! He's safe with me, I promise you that! In my war, he's as safe as safe can be!"

"Maybe in your war, yes."

That was the problem. Mister Superspeed's war was not the same war as Albie's.

Linus closed Albie's notebook and slid it back onto the pile with the others. As he tied the string around the newspaper, he kept his weight on the package, as if he was scared that Mister Superspeed might slip out.

Linus slid the two parcels under the bed and into the corner.

Albie's war was a real war. So real that it scared Linus.

25

THE ORANGES SEEMED TO weigh twice as much as usual. In fact, Linus's miserable mood of the past few days made everything feel heavier. Slowly, he made his way up the stairs.

"Hello, Linus." The door swung open before Linus had reached the top. "Come on in."

Linus hesitated.

"Or don't you have the time today?" Mr. Orange looked at him. "Is everything all right? You've not had bad news about your brother, I hope."

"No, not about Albie," said Linus. "But about his friend, who was also from around here, and now he's… he's dead." He put down the crate with a thud. "Stone dead, and it's all because of the war." The harshness of his own words startled him. But at the same time he wanted them to sound harsh. It felt good.

"That's wretched," Mr. Orange said quietly. "This whole rotten war is wretched." He bent down to pick up two oranges from the crate and started coughing.

"The wicked witch, that's what I call the war." He carefully stood up straight. "Like the queen in *Snow White*, she's hard to beat because she knows so many mean tricks."

Linus followed him into the kitchen. Two plates were out on the table, ready and waiting. Mr. Orange had been expecting him, as usual. His miserable mood was beginning to lift a little. He sat down on a stool. The door to the studio was slightly open. He breathed in the smell of paint.

"And yet fighting back is our only option." Mr. Orange sat down opposite him. "We have to keep on resisting."

"But you left," Linus blurted out. It was a thought that had been buzzing around his head for a while, so he didn't regret saying it. Mr. Orange nodded. He didn't seem at all upset by Linus's words.

"Everyone fights in his own way. Your brother is young and strong, so he can fight with muscle power. But an old man like me?" He smiled a small, wry smile. "The enemy would walk all over me." The knife sliced into the orange. Halves, quarters, eighths. "All I have to depend on is my imagination."

"Imagination?" The word shook Linus. His miserable mood suddenly returned. "What good is imagination in a war? Imagination can't stop bullets. Not real ones."

"Ah!" Mr. Orange waved his knife. "Make no mistake! Imagination is a powerful weapon." His eyes were gleaming.

He just doesn't understand, thought Linus. *He's here in this wonderful place with his paintings, while over in Europe real soldiers are dying, and he's just, just...*

"Imagining things, making them up—it's all just hiding!" Linus shouted. "Hiding from everything that's real—the war, the bullets, the wounded soldiers." Why was he so angry with Mr. Orange? *If I carry on like this, I'll have to explain to Dad why Mr. Orange has canceled his order*, thought Linus. *The customer's always right*. His father's voice echoed somewhere in the back of his mind, but he couldn't stop. He raced on, as if he were riding downhill in his cart without a brake. There was a canyon at the bottom of the hill and he was heading straight for it, faster and faster. No one could save him now. No one except Mister Superspeed, who would throw himself in front of the cart, turn up his steam to full power, and stop him with one hand without even knocking his helmet askew. But he'd sent Mister Superspeed away, and it was just as well because the very thought of him made Linus even angrier.

"Everything here is so wonderful," he said, pointing at the studio. "But it's so…" He tried to find the right word. Somewhere outside a car honked. "It's so far away from everything. When I'm here, I can almost believe that the real world doesn't exist."

Mr. Orange continued to peel the oranges. His face didn't show what he was thinking.

"You talk about Snow White and wicked witches… But they belong in fairy tales." *Just like superheroes*, Linus thought. "They only exist in the imagination."

"But imagination is so much more than that!" Mr. Orange pushed the plate of orange slices across the table to Linus. Strangely enough, he didn't seem angry at all.

"Imagination isn't only about things that don't really exist. Imagination is exactly what you need to make real things." He gave Linus a big smile. "New things. Things that don't exist and then suddenly do, all because someone sees a possibility and invents them. It all starts with imagination. It's the first step in everything that human beings have ever made."

He waved his hand around him. "Everything that you see here in the city, inside and outside, everything that you can touch and point to and hold on to, everything that you call 'real'—all of it started in somebody's head, as an idea. Without imagination, none of this would exist." He pointed outside. "No streets, no buildings, no city." His cheeks were glowing as though he had a fever.

"This table." He knocked on it. "This house." He stamped his foot on the floor. "All of it perfectly solid, all of it real. And all of it is real because of the imagination. That's how powerful imagination is."

Mr. Orange looked at Linus as though all of this was perfectly obvious. Linus picked at a piece of orange.

"I still don't understand what it's all got to do with the war. I mean…" Linus hesitated, but he simply had to ask the question. "What about your paintings? A bit of paint on a canvas is never going to win a war, is it?"

"If imagination were as harmless as you think," said Mr. Orange, "then the Nazis wouldn't be so scared of it."

"Scared? The Nazis?"

"Hard to believe, eh? Scared of a bit of paint on a canvas," said Mr. Orange with a mocking tone. "In fact, they're so scared that they just might ban my paintings."

"Ban them?"

Mr. Orange smiled at Linus's surprise. "Like the work of so many others. Like everything else that isn't up their alley. What they'd really like to do is to silence everyone who doesn't share their opinions." He smiled again, but it was a sad smile. "If it weren't so awful, one might almost feel proud."

"So that's why you had to leave… because you were in danger!" Linus held his breath. "Were you scared?"

"Not for myself." Mr. Orange waved his words away. "I was scared for my work. Scared that I wouldn't be allowed to make any more paintings, scared that no one would ever see them. Then they would have won." He coughed. "Fortunately,

I knew some people who could help me come to New York. Here I'm free to make whatever I want."

The coughing was so bad that he had to stop talking. He stood up, filled a glass of water and stood by the sink as he drank it. He looked much too flushed. *Maybe I should leave*, thought Linus. But Mr. Orange came and sat down with him again.

"Painting is *my* way of fighting back." He was talking as though nothing had happened. "It's my way of trying to find out how things might be better in the future."

"The future?" Linus pushed his empty plate as far away as he could, as though that might push the word away, too. "What does the future matter, as long as we're still in the middle of the war?"

"Winning the war is the same thing as fighting for the future," said Mr. Orange. "A future where people have their freedom and are allowed to say what they believe and to have an opinion of their own."

"What if we lose?" asked Linus.

"That's not going to happen."

"How can you be so sure?"

"I have every confidence." Mr. Orange looked at him calmly through those dark glasses of his. "Whenever people have their freedom taken away, they always fight back. Sooner or later." He made a fist and put up his forefinger and middle finger to make a V.

"V for Victory." His smile made him look almost boyish. "Did you know that now it's forbidden even to make that sign?"

Linus clenched his fist, imitating the gesture.

"Winning the war," said Mr. Orange, "means making sure that the imagination remains free. And that's the most important thing of all."

"So in fact," said Linus slowly, "Albie's working just as hard for the future as you are... He's actually fighting so that you can go on painting."

"Absolutely." Mr. Orange put his hands flat on the table and pushed himself up. "And so that you can look at it... when it's finished. Which means that I need to get back to work."

As they walked to the door, Mr. Orange rested his hand on Linus's shoulder. "When it's done, you'll be able to see what I mean, without all these words..." He sighed, as though the conversation had tired him out. The sigh made him start coughing again.

"Until next time," he whispered, raising his hand to wave goodbye.

Linus waved back and headed down the stairs. He couldn't wait to see what the future was going to look like. Or at least the future that Mr. Orange was trying to find.

26

Castelli's was busy. So busy that Linus had come around after dinner to make an extra delivery. Even with the door closed behind him, he could still hear people laughing and talking inside. He breathed in the frosty air. It was after eight and the streets were quiet. The snow that had been gathering in the sky all day had finally started to fall. A thin layer of white already lay on the sidewalk. The snow was so fresh that there still were hardly any tracks in it.

The wheels of the empty cart slipped a little in the soft snow. Linus stopped at the corner. The shortest way home was straight ahead. But Bartali's delicatessen was straight ahead too… He thought he could even see the sign from where he stood. He'd been avoiding that part of the street recently.

Linus pushed back his cap and lifted his face. The white snowflakes stood out against the dark sky. He closed his eyes for a moment. He couldn't keep steering clear of the delicatessen forever, could he?

The snowflakes fell gently on his forehead and were cold on his cheeks. He took a deep breath and crossed the street. Before long, he was able to clearly see the sign on the other side of the street, emerging from the snowflakes.

There was nothing special about the building. It was late and the store had been closed for a while. Now that he'd come this far, he thought he might as well cross the street.

There was the pennant with the two stars.

Two stars, but only one of them was blue.

The other star was now gold. A gold star was for families who had lost someone in the war.

Such a beautiful thing, Linus thought, his eyes glued to the star. *Such a beautiful thing for something so terrible.*

He couldn't stop staring at it.

Because of the snow, he didn't hear the footsteps until they were very close. They stopped at the door of the delicatessen, right beside Linus.

The footsteps belonged to a soldier. Most likely, Gervasio's brother. His uniform looked like Albie's. The soldier took a key from his pocket and opened the door. Before he went inside, he looked over at Linus. Giving him a quick nod, he said good evening. His father must have taught him the same lesson as Linus's father: always be polite, because anyone could be a customer. The door closed before Linus could respond.

Quietly, he walked on, the cart sliding on the snow as he went. He wished he'd said something to the soldier, made some friendly remark, but of course the soldier had no idea who he was. And anyway, what could he have said? What could you say to someone who had lost his brother? Inside his head, it was silent, as silent as the street, where the snow muffled every sound.

Linus looked through the window and saw that his father was in the store. He wasn't surprised to see him downstairs in the evening, but his father didn't usually sit on a crate like that, staring into the distance. He was perfectly still, with his hands in his lap. Linus tapped on the window.

His father stood up and came over to let him in. He helped Linus brush the snow off the cart, but he didn't say anything. Linus pulled the cart through to the back, and when he put his head around the corner to say goodnight, he saw that his father had pulled up another crate. His dad gestured for him to come over, put his hand into his jacket pocket and took out a familiar piece of paper.

"Did you read the letter from Albie?" he asked, without waiting for Linus to sit down.

Linus was startled. How did his father know?

"You don't need to be a detective to figure it out." His father pointed at the bloodstain that Linus had tried to wipe off.

Linus nodded. He clenched his fists in his pockets and prepared himself for the lecture that was sure to follow.

His father leaned forward, his elbows on his knees, and stared at the envelope. He kept turning it over and over in his hands, as if he thought he might find the words he wanted to say written on it.

Linus studied him carefully, out of the corner of one eye. He didn't look angry. He just looked… different. Linus couldn't quite work out his expression.

"This letter wasn't meant for you," his father finally said. He turned his head toward Linus, but didn't actually look at him. "Linus, I'm worried."

"About Albie?" Linus nodded. So was he.

His father shook his head. "About you."

"About me?" Linus stared at him. What had happened to the lecture?

"I'm worried about how you might have taken Albie's news." He coughed. "It's bad news, about his friend."

Linus nodded. "I just walked by their store," he said. "There's a gold star in the window."

The envelope kept on turning, over and over and over. Linus wasn't sure his father had heard him.

"But it doesn't mean anything's going to happen to Albie," his father said very slowly. His voice sounded strange. "Albie's doing just fine."

"The war is wretched," said Linus.

"Wretched?" His father made a sound as though he was about to laugh, but then he stopped himself. "What a strange word."

"That's what Mr. Orange says," Linus explained. "That the war is wretched, and that…"

"It doesn't mean anything's going to happen to Albie," his father repeated, "and we mustn't forget that." Linus was upset to see how deep the lines on his father's forehead had become. Suddenly he knew the word for his father's expression. It was fear. His father was scared, just like he was. He could tell by the lines, and by the way his father wouldn't give him a straight look. He was scared of what hadn't happened but might happen. Scared of what their mother wouldn't let him say out loud.

Linus leaped to his feet. He didn't want a father who was worried. He wanted a father who said everything was going to turn out fine. With Albie, with the war, with their victory. A father who had every confidence that they would win, just like Mr. Orange. He walked up and down from the counter to his father and back again, and he did his best to remember Mr. Orange's words. How had he put it?

"Mr. Orange says you need imagination to win the war."

"Imagination?" His father pulled his eyebrows into one single bristly line. Linus hesitated. When Mr. Orange had said it, it had all sounded so logical, but now he didn't feel quite so sure.

"All of the things that don't exist yet... Well, we have to imagine them first, before they can become real." Was that what he'd said? Linus was confused.

His father seemed to be losing interest.

"I don't mean like a trick or anything, I mean..." Frantically, he searched for the right words. "I mean that Albie's gone to war because he has imagination." He sat down, surprised by his own thought. His father's eyebrows shot up so high that they almost reached his hair.

"If he couldn't have imagined that we'd win the war, he'd never have gone!" Now the words were coming by themselves. "He went because he could imagine the future. The right future. I mean, not the future where everyone has to do what the enemy wants, but the other future. The future where we're free to think and choose for ourselves. That's why he went to fight. Because he understood that it's something worth fighting for."

His father's eyebrows were still raised in surprise.

"And if Albie can imagine that we'll win, while the bullets are whistling around his ears..." He paused. What should he say next? "Well, then it can't be too hard for us to imagine the same thing, can it? And that Albie will come home safe?" Linus felt really warm now.

His father's eyebrows were back where they belonged, and

the beginnings of a smile hovered around his mouth. Finally, his father looked at him.

"You're a funny one, Linus Gregor Muller." His father looked at him for a long time, with his keen, thoughtful eyes. It almost made him feel shy. And why did he have to use his middle name like that?

His father laid a hand on his head, ruffled his hair, and let his hand rest there for a moment before slowly standing up. Then he walked over to the shop window and, as he rolled down the blind, he quietly whistled a tune. When the blind was halfway down, he looked around at Linus, shook his head, and smiled slowly.

Linus stood up, relieved. Not because he'd managed to escape a lecture, but because he no longer had to keep the letter a secret.

His father turned out the light in the store.

"Oh, yes." He stopped at the bottom of the stairs and turned around to look at Linus. "Just remember, the next time you feel tempted to read mail that isn't meant for your eyes, you'll be cleaning beets and carrots every Saturday afternoon for a year."

Linus nodded, pleased that he was getting off with a warning.

"This time it will just be four Saturdays." His father couldn't help smiling again when he saw the face Linus pulled. "Not a day less—and there's no point trying to bargain with me."

27

"What on earth are you doing?"

Caught by surprise, Linus looked up. His father was standing behind the counter with his hands on his hips, staring at him. Linus had just moved some potatoes into a different box and repacked the potato box with oranges. It was an extra-strong one, just the sort of box that he knew Mr. Orange would be able to put to good use.

"Your cart's in the way. The customers can't get in through the door." His father frowned, but his eyes looked more amused than angry. Life at home had become more cheerful again lately.

"I'm ready to go!" Linus picked up the potato box, now full of oranges, and started to carry it through the store. He was just about to tell his father what he'd been doing with the boxes when he saw the mailman trying to squeeze past his cart. Linus put down the oranges in the middle of the aisle so that he could go and move the cart.

"Never mind!" The mailman reached over the cart and handed him an envelope. "Will you just give this to your dad, eh?" He tapped his cap and nodded through the window at Linus's father.

"Mr. and Mrs. A. Muller," was written in typed letters on the envelope. There was a big postmark in the top corner. Linus could just make out the words "Department" and "War." News about Albie? But it wasn't from Albie himself... Linus handed the letter to his father and looked at him, hoping for an answer.

His father stared at the envelope before dropping it onto the counter, as though it had burned his fingers.

"Go get your mother," he said stiffly. He walked around the counter and locked the door. "And stay upstairs."

"But..."

"Now!" His father turned around abruptly, stumbling over the box in the aisle. Oranges rolled in every direction. He didn't even seem to notice.

Linus flew upstairs, taking two steps at a time.

His mother took one look at his face and said, "Take care of the little ones, Linus. Max is running an errand." She hurried down the stairs.

Linus stood frozen in the doorway. An official letter about Albie... it couldn't be good news. He held his breath and tried to hear what was going on downstairs, but the little ones were making too much noise. Willy was chasing Sis around the table. Willy was growling and Sis was squealing. Linus went over and picked up Sis. She squealed even louder and kicked her little legs in protest.

"Shhh." Linus sat down at the table with Sis on his lap. Oddly enough, she sat still as well and stared at him with her big eyes. Willy kept running around the table, as though he hadn't even noticed that Sis had stopped playing with him.

Linus took a deep breath and waited. He felt a little better with Sis on his lap. As long as he held onto her, nothing bad could happen, could it?

Finally, he heard footsteps coming up the stairs. Their father appeared in the doorway first, his face strangely white. Their mother's eyes were rimmed with red. Willy stopped running and came and stood beside Linus. The three children looked at their mother, then at their father, and back again.

"We've had a letter about Albie," said their father. His voice sounded as though he had a cold. Linus squeezed Sis tight, his eyes glued to their father's face. A smile briefly flashed across it, but it disappeared just as quickly as it came. So quickly that Linus thought he might have imagined it.

"He's coming home soon."

The words hung in the middle of the room.

"Is the war over now?" Willy asked, breaking the silence.

Their father shook his head.

"He's coming home because he's sick." Again that smile that immediately hid itself, like the sun behind the clouds on a windy day.

"Is Albie hurt?" Willy piped up again. Linus held his breath. He didn't know how Willy dared to ask the question. Wasn't he scared to hear the answer?

"He's not hurt, but his feet are sick. They couldn't cope with the wet and the cold in the Italian mountains. It's called trench foot. Lots of soldiers get it. Albie's case is serious, but with proper care it can heal just fine. There's a ship coming home soon with wounded and sick soldiers, and Albie's going to be on it."

No one said anything. They didn't seem to know whether they should be happy or not.

"Ow!" Sis struggled out of Linus's grip and slid off his lap. It wasn't until Linus tried to stand up that he realized how weak his arms and legs felt.

There was banging on the door downstairs.

"Customers! They won't give you a moment's rest." This time, the smile stayed on their father's face a little longer. He kissed their mother on the cheek and looked at Linus. "Would you move the cart out of the way?"

Linus followed his father. Downstairs in the store, he stood there feeling dazed as he stared at the oranges scattered over the floor.

"If you pick them up, Linus, I'll go and let our hungry customers in." He picked his way through the oranges to the door. His father's own, familiar voice had come back. That helped, and Linus found that he could move normally again.

28

ALBIE'S COMING HOME!

Linus pushed open the door onto the street. It had only just dawned on him how long it had been since he'd last seen him. When his big brother went away, it was September. Now it was February.

The strange thing about waiting for something, thought Linus, *is that the closer it comes, the harder it is to be patient.* As he loaded the box onto the cart, he imagined seeing Albie again for the first time. Maybe it would be when he got back from making his deliveries. Down the block, on the other side of the street, a person would suddenly catch his eye. And of course he'd immediately recognize Albie's familiar figure, with his kitbag on his shoulder. Linus felt the corners of his mouth moving toward his ears into a grin that was wider than his face. "Albie!" he would shout as loud as he could, and everyone would come racing outside.

But he doesn't shout out loud. Instead, as usual, he leaves the cart in front of the window below the blue star and walks toward him. Albie spots him immediately, and they start to cross the street at the same time. He starts to run and meets Albie halfway. He'd love to leap into his arms, but of course that's not what he does.

He stops right in front of him, in the middle of the street, and thumps his arm. The second thump lands on Albie's stomach, which he tenses up hard as only he can, so Linus's sledgehammer blow won't hurt him. Linus now has no choice but to start tickling Albie until he's laughing so much that he can't keep his stomach muscles tensed, and Linus can slam his head into his stomach. Even then, Albie still can't stop laughing, so he hooks his arm around Linus's neck and locks him in a wrestling hold, and they spin around and around. Cars honk as they drive past, but he and Albie ignore them. They continue to spin until Linus has to beg for mercy and Albie finally lets go. They stand there together, dizzy from all the laughing and the spinning.

But hold on, if Albie has bad feet, he won't be walking… Even so, Linus couldn't resist taking a look over his shoulder, just in case. Then he grabbed his cart and quickly went on his way, walking with big steps as if that might help the time to pass more quickly.

He stopped on the corner at Third Avenue, on Liam's block, and looked left to see if he could spot Liam with that mean MacKenna. For the first time, the thought didn't make him angry. He suddenly couldn't imagine not being friends with Liam anymore. All of his anger seemed to have seeped away. Before he could change his mind, he'd turned the corner and was heading down the block.

He started calling out Liam's name before he'd even reached his house. He banged on the door and called again. As loud as he could. Upstairs a window slid open and Liam's surprised face looked out. He didn't say anything, just disappeared inside. Linus waited. He heard the familiar thud of feet on the stairs, and then the door flew open. Liam came out with his cap on, his coat still in his hands. They stood looking at each other, a little awkwardly.

Liam pretended he was busy putting his coat on.

"Albie's coming home," said Linus.

"Really?" said Liam. A grin spread across his face. "That's swell!"

He put his hands in his pockets and kicked a stone down the sidewalk.

"That Georgie's a moron," he said.

"You just realized? I could have told you that ages ago."

"Yeah, you did," said Liam with a wry smile. He pushed his hands even deeper into his pockets. "Rosie dumped him."

"I knew she was a smart girl."

"That's going a bit far." Liam grinned. "Anyway, it took her long enough."

Yeah, you too, thought Linus. He kicked a pebble. It hit a lamppost and bounced back, landing neatly in front of his feet. They both burst out laughing.

"I have to go deliver some oranges," said Linus.

"Want me to come with you?" asked Liam.

Linus hesitated. He wasn't sure Mr. Orange would like that.

"I'll come by on the way back," he said, giving Liam a thump on the arm.

"Don't forget." Liam thumped him back hard. *Ow, that's going to bruise*, thought Linus happily. He turned the cart around and walked back up the street. When he glanced back, Liam was still standing there. Linus grinned and waved as he went around the corner.

The box didn't seem to weigh anything as he walked up the stairs at Mr. Orange's. Before long, he'd be able to lift it with one hand, and he'd be able to show Albie how good he was at lifting. *Maybe,* he thought, *I can even introduce Albie to Mr. Orange!* Mister Orange had heard lots about Albie, after all, and they both had made the same ocean crossing...

The door upstairs was still closed. Linus knocked.Albie was sure to enjoy meeting Mr. Orange. They could talk about Europe, about drawing... He would ask Mr. Orange now if he thought that would be nice. No—he'd make it a surprise! They would just show up, the two of them. Maybe even the next time Linus was due to come.

The door swings open, and Mr. Orange looks at them through his dark-rimmed glasses, surprised but amused, with his little smile.

"Mr. Orange, this is my brother Albie. He's just come home from the war. Albie, this is Mr. Orange, he comes from Europe and is a painter." They shake hands.

"Albie wants to be an artist," Linus says, casually dropping it into the conversation.

"Ah," says Mr. Orange. "That's enormous!"

Maybe he can help Albie. Why not? Maybe he can even teach him...

"Yes?"

Linus hadn't noticed that the door had opened. A man he didn't know was looking at him with a quizzical expression. He had a camera around his neck. A big one, the kind that Linus had seen the newspaper photographers walking around with on the morning of the military parade all those months ago. An eternity ago.

"Delivery for Mr. Orange," said Linus, nodding at the crate that he was clutching to his stomach.

"Mr. Orange?" The man looked suspiciously at Linus and

then at the oranges. "Is that supposed to be a joke?" He started to close the door.

"No, no, not at all!" Linus shouted quickly. Why couldn't he ever remember Mr. Orange's real name? "I'm the delivery boy."

"We don't need any deliveries here," the man said sharply. "Just take your box and go."

"Who's that?" Footsteps came closer.

"Some boy trying to be a wise guy," the man shouted back. Linus recognized the face that now appeared.

"Hello there, orange boy," said the man Mr. Orange had called Harry. He smiled, but he didn't look very happy. "What my friend here is trying to say is that, well... most unfortunately your Mr. Orange got very sick."

"Sick? Mr. Orange?" Just as well, then, that he'd brought plenty of fresh oranges for him.

"He had to go to the hospital because he had severe pneumonia and, well... sadly, he didn't make it."

Linus didn't understand. What didn't he make?

"He died last week." Harry was looking down at his feet. "There was nothing they could do for him at the hospital."

"Last week?" Linus shook his head. It couldn't possibly be true. Not of Mr. Orange. He still had to tell him about Albie. He looked at the closed kitchen door.

How could he be dead when they'd been sitting there only the other day, talking about the war and about the future? Linus stared at the oranges. What was going to happen to the future now?

"I'll send someone around to settle the account," said Harry. He gave him a friendly nod.

Linus slowly turned around. Behind him he heard the

door close with a click. He walked down the stairs, clutching the crate so tightly that his arms started to cramp up. He'd packed it up specially that afternoon because he'd thought that Mr. Orange would be able to use it.

The crate! He stopped at the foot of the stairs. He thought about the cupboard made of orange boxes, about the table Mr. Orange had built himself, about the walls covered with colored shapes, about the music—about all of the things that were part of Mr. Orange's bright and cheerful world. He remembered the men whistling as they emptied Mrs. De Winter's apartment. He thought about her things on the sidewalk in the pouring rain.

Linus put the crate down and raced back up the stairs. He hammered on the door until he heard footsteps coming.

"What's going to happen to everything?" he shouted before the door was even open.

"Everything?" Harry looked impatient now.

"All of Mr. Orange's things, his bits and pieces, the furniture he made… You're not going to throw it all out onto the street, are you?"

"Onto the street?" Harry started to laugh. "Not a chance! We're not throwing out a single thing, I promise you. We'll take very good care of it all."

Linus heaved a sigh of relief.

"But it's kind of you to be so concerned." Harry took a long look at him and his expression seemed friendlier now.

"Would you like to come in and take one last look?" he asked.

Linus thought about the diamond-shaped painting. He wondered if Mr. Orange had managed to finish it. Maybe he could see it now…

So, how do you like it? The thought of Mr. Orange's half-smile made Linus sad. He shook his head.

"No thanks, I'd rather not. Not now," he said. Not without Mr. Orange. He walked to the stairs. Harry stood in the doorway, watching him. He didn't seem to be in a hurry now.

"My brother's coming home. From the war." Linus didn't know why he'd suddenly blurted that out to someone who knew nothing about Albie.

"That's good news." Harry smiled.

Linus was glad that he'd said it out loud. Even though Mr. Orange wasn't there to hear it.

"What's his name?" he heard a voice saying behind him. "This brother of yours."

"Albie." Linus stopped halfway down the stairs. "Actually, Albert," he added, catching himself. "He likes us to call him Albert."

"Well, congratulations. Give him my best wishes." Harry waved and went back inside. Linus stood watching until the door had shut.

It's strange, he thought as he went down the stairs, *the way good news can come at the same time as terrible news.* Wouldn't it be much better to get all of the bad news out of the way all at once? Then it would be possible to feel truly happy about the good news.

At the bottom of the stairs he tripped over the crate. He hadn't seen it because his eyes were now filled with useless tears. *Have you very much hurt yourself?* Mr. Orange's odd choice of words shot through his mind, the words he'd said the very first time Linus had come. He could almost hear them echoing around the empty hallway. Linus scrambled to his feet, gave his eyes a good wipe and picked up the crate.

It was already getting dark outside.

Don't look up, Linus told himself, but his eyes wouldn't listen. The lights were on in the windows above the shop. From down there, everything still looked normal, just the same as ever. From down there, it was as though he could still hear the music... Snatches of it danced through his head. He could picture Mr. Orange hopping across the room like a skinny bird. But this time it didn't make him smile. It just made him feel empty. He turned around, walked down the street, and rounded the corner. The crate of oranges bounced in the cart.

He was almost at Liam's corner when he remembered his promise.

I'm going to Liam's! His happiness about their fight being over flooded through him. Thoughts of Albie naturally followed.

Albie's coming home!

Now the snatches of music in his head were starting to make him feel better. His feet began to move to the beat, dancing one step and then another. *Too much hip!* Mr. Orange would have shouted if he could have seen him.

Linus let go of the cart, put his hands on his hips to keep them still, and tried again.

"Hey, look at Linus go! He's wearing his dancing shoes!" Rosie was leaning out of the upstairs window.

Linus ignored her and did the same steps again, and then again. Let Rosie laugh if she wanted. If he wanted to dance, he'd dance. *If I had paint on the soles of my shoes,* he thought, *I could dance a painting on the sidewalk.*

"Liam! You have a visitor!" Rosie yelled. "And he's as crazy as a bedbug!"

Linus heard thudding on the stairs. As he waited for Liam, he looked up and gave a bow. Rosie applauded.

Downstairs, the door opened.

NEW YORK
MARCH 1945

WHAT WERE YOU EXPECTING? says Linus to his reflection. He says it without moving his lips. He doesn't want all the people here thinking he's as crazy as a bedbug.

The windows of the building are gleaming so brightly that he can't see what's inside. All he can see are the reflections of the people who are heading past him to the entrance—men in winter coats and shiny shoes and ladies in furs and elegant hats. They walk in through the glass doors as if it's their home. There's a buzz of excitement in the air.

The spring sunshine streams between two tall buildings into the street. Linus can feel the warmth on his back. He tilts his head and looks up. The white of the roof stands out against the brilliant blue of the sky. Almost the entire front of the building is made of glass. With its sleek façade, it looks like something from the future. Mr. Orange would be happy.

Linus lets his gaze slide all the way down the glass until he's once again looking himself in the eye. *What were you expecting? That you'd find your Mr. Orange here?*

He gives a tiny shrug. After all, Mr. Orange doesn't belong to him. He knows that. Here, Mr. Orange is a man with a name that Linus can never remember, a man who has made paintings that all of these men and women have come to see. He had no idea that so many people were just as curious about Mr. Orange as he is.

His gaze moves on, over his old winter jacket to his feet. Even though his shoes fit perfectly now, they still don't look great. Not stylish enough to walk through those spotlessly gleaming doors.

The sun disappears behind the building as quickly as it came. Linus shivers. He puts his hands in his pockets and hunches his shoulders. Maybe going down to the river was a better idea after all... Maybe it still is. If he runs, he'll be there in no time. Linus takes a step back and turns around, bumping straight into a group of people who are smoking by the entrance.

"Hey, watch where you're going!" The man he bumped into grabs him by the shoulders. They recognize each other at the same moment.

"Orange boy!" The man Mr. Orange called Harry looks surprised to see Linus, but he's smiling. "How nice that you've come to take a look. What did you think?"

Linus mumbles something. He can feel his cheeks turning red.

"Oh, haven't you been inside yet?"

Linus looks down at his feet.

"Great!" Harry drops his cigarette to the ground and stamps it out. "Then I'll go in with you and show you around. See you later," he says to his friends. With his hand still on Linus's shoulder, he steers him through the glass doors and into the building. Sunlight streams in through the gleaming windows, and men with one hand tucked behind their backs walk around with trays full of drinks. Harry walks so quickly that Linus can barely keep up with him. He nips through the crowd, nodding and saying hello to people as he goes. He seems to know everyone. Then he says something to Linus, but Linus can't hear him because his ears are ringing from all the laughter and chatter. They weave through the rooms, turning around one corner and then another. Finally, they stop in a large white room. Surprised, Linus hears himself gasp.

There it is! Straight ahead, at the other end of the room. He doesn't feel at all uncomfortable now. He pushes through the crowd and heads straight for it, stopping just a couple of feet away.

"The last painting he worked on." Harry comes and stands beside him.

Linus nods. He recognizes it by its shape. A square with one of its corners pointing up like a diamond. The painting he'd seen only from behind.

Someone comes over to speak to Harry and pulls him away. Linus hardly notices. He takes another step forward. It's the strangest painting he's ever seen, and yet he feels as though he already knows it.

Small and large areas of color move around, chasing one another. They almost seem to be falling over themselves with impatience. Blocks of yellow, red, and blue dance with white and gray, swirling and swaying to the music. But no... they *are* the music. They move closer and then apart, as though they are performing some complicated dance. Everything changes as Linus looks at the painting, and yet it's as if each element has its own place, and no single block of color ever gets lost. Wherever he looks, it all fits together perfectly.

It's as if the painting opens up a door, thinks Linus. *As if it draws you into a different world, shakes you up, and hurls you back out into your own, and suddenly that world looks just a little bit different.*

He doesn't have to try too hard to imagine Mr. Orange beside the painting, with his head at that slight tilt, his invisible smile twitching at the corner of his mouth.

Linus takes a step closer.

So, how do you like it?

Now he can see the colored pieces of tape all over the canvas. The longer he looks, the more tape he discovers—little strips are stuck all over the painting, most of them precisely, but some look a bit untidy, as if Mr. Orange had been in a hurry.

It makes Linus think of the colored shapes on Mr. Orange's white walls, and of all of the nail holes around them. *It's all about searching… It's a bit like a puzzle…* Linus starts to laugh. He can't help it. A gallery attendant turns around and glares at him. Linus rubs his hands over his cheeks and takes deep breaths, trying to make his face look serious again.

It's as if Mr. Orange was just here a minute ago, Linus thinks. As if he had just been puzzling away at the canvas with his pieces of tape, completely absorbed in his work… As if he'd walked away just now, maybe because someone was at the door. Someone with a crate of oranges… *Linus! Come in. I was expecting you…*

Linus spots a label on the wall beside the painting and smiles when he reads the name: *Victory Boogie-Woogie*.

V for Victory… Linus can still see Mr. Orange making a fist, and then raising two slender fingers into a triumphant V.

In recent months, there have been more and more reports saying that the war in Europe will soon be over. Mr. Orange made this painting when the war was still raging, and yet, on his canvas, the war was already over. That's how confident he'd been of victory. *Just like Albie*, thinks Linus. Albie, who had come home from the war last year, but had gone right back just as soon as he'd recovered.

Suddenly Mister Superspeed pops into Linus's head. It's strange because it's been ages since he last thought about him. Why, in an important museum like this, would he be thinking about such a, such a…

"… such a useless superhero? A product of the imagination? You know, the kind of imagination that won't help win any wars?"

Linus turns. Mister Superspeed is leaning against the wall, his muscular arms folded across his chest. Pushing himself forward, Mister Superspeed walks over to Linus.

"That man certainly understood color." He hooks his thumbs into his belt and sticks out his chest. "It's no wonder his work reminded you of me." Pushing back his helmet, Mister Superspeed leans forward. That's way too close, Linus thinks nervously. Mister Superspeed's nose is practically touching the painting.

"Somehow, this seems familiar." Mister Superspeed taps the glass in front of the painting thoughtfully. Linus looks around, but no one else has noticed.

Then Mister Superspeed's face lights up. "I know—it reminds me of the city when I fly over it. It's what the buildings look like from above, and all the streets with the lines of cars crossing at the corners…" He turns his ear toward the painting. "I can almost hear them blowing their horns."

Linus laughs again. It's bubbling out of him. It's so good to see Mister Superspeed. He opens his mouth to say something, but then there's a bang outside, followed by the honking of car horns. Some of the visitors wander over to the windows.

"That sounds like a job for me," says Mister Superspeed, rubbing his hands together. He straightens his helmet and clicks his heels together, making steam puff out of his boots. He shoots up into the air. Before Linus can say anything, Mister Superspeed has vanished. For a moment, a small cloud of steam seems to hang where he was just standing.

I haven't lost Mr. Orange at all, thinks Linus. He turns back to the painting. Everything he remembers about Mr. Orange is there.

I've finally managed to get boogie-woogie into it!

Is he really hearing music, or is it just in his head? Linus isn't sure, but it doesn't matter. It's the music he can remember only short snatches of, but it has so much swing that his toes start to tap and his cheeks start to glow. Suddenly, he just can't stand still. His legs begin to move, and then his arms join in.

The gallery attendant is nowhere in sight.

Two women standing in front of the next painting turn to look at him. One of them purses her lips. She turns around and walks off. The other raises her eyebrows, interested. Her dress is exactly the right shade of blue. Mr. Orange's kind of blue.

She stands watching Linus for a moment before following her friend. As she walks off, she does a couple of little dance steps. Then she looks over her shoulder and smiles. She seems to be dancing to the very same beat. Maybe the music isn't only in his head...

Keep those hips still!

Linus taps his toes and smiles back.

MISTER MONDRIAN

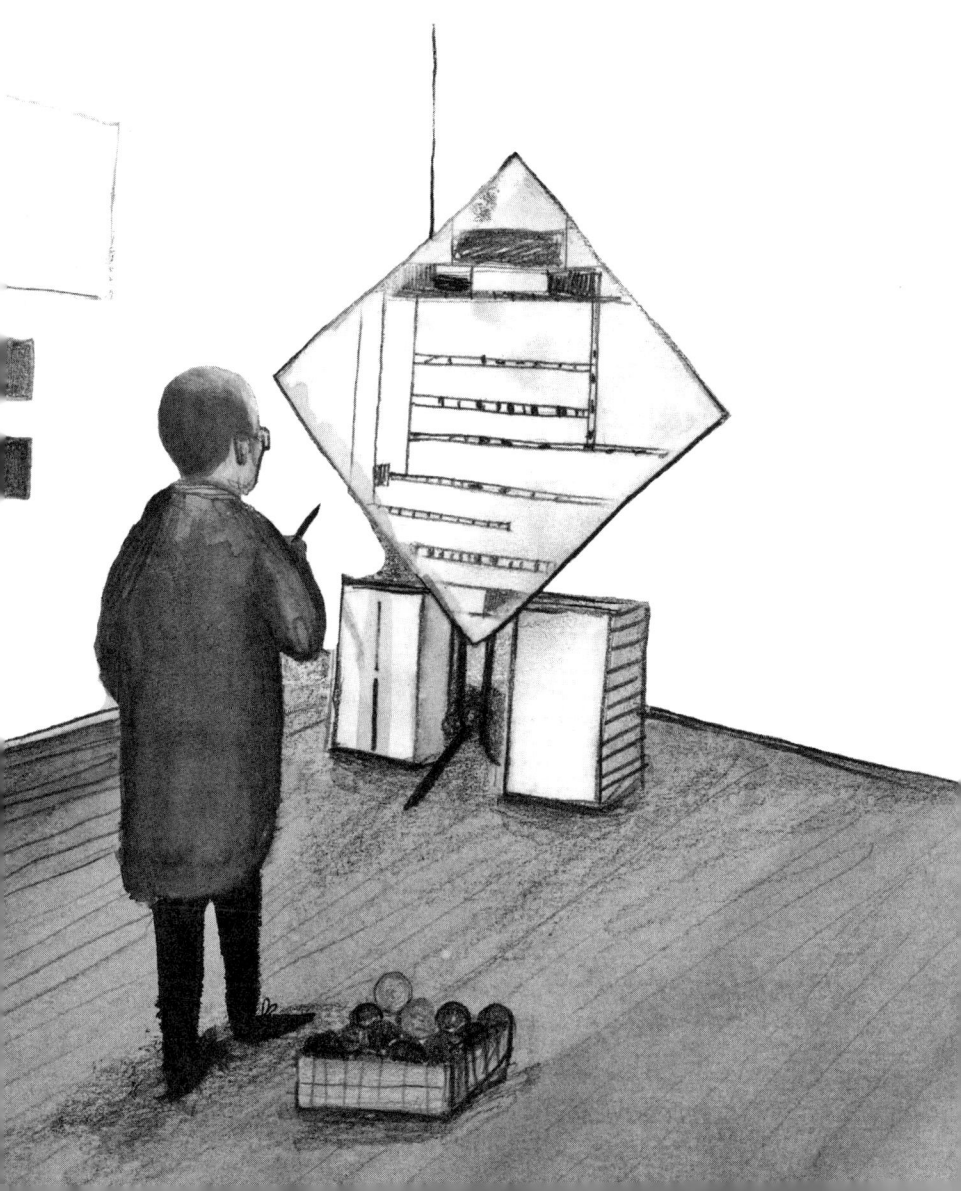

Boogie-Woogie in New York
Piet Mondrian (1872–1944), on whom the character of Mr. Orange is based, was always searching for new ways to paint. Instead of painting in a familiar or traditional style, he wanted to make paintings that looked completely new and unlike anything else. Shape, color, rhythm: he wanted to balance all of these elements and to keep his work interesting. His art had to have life! He wanted people to have a strong reaction when they looked at his paintings, the way people often do when they see a movie or listen to music.

Mondrian tried out all kinds of different things. After a while, he decided to work only with the primary colors: red, yellow, and blue. And the lines he painted always had to run horizontally or vertically. He invented many more rules for himself to help in his search for a new way to paint. But whenever his own rules got in the way, he soon changed those, too.

Eventually, Mondrian's paintings became famous all over the world. His work has given new ideas to many people in many different fields, and every year millions of people flock to museums to see his paintings.

was replace the tape with paint. However, once he'd done that, he often couldn't resist the temptation to try out something new, and soon his painting would be covered with tape again. Just as he kept on experimenting and moving the colored shapes on his walls, he also continued to explore in his painting. What he wanted more than anything was to make the very best painting he could.

Even when he got sick with pneumonia and had a high fever, Mondrian continued to work in his pajamas until he was so ill that he had to be taken to the hospital. He died there on February 1, 1944. His last painting remained in his studio, completely covered with new pieces of tape, some of which he had attached only days before.

Moving into the Future
It doesn't happen very often that we see a painting in a museum that is really famous even though it isn't finished. Mondrian wanted his *Victory Boogie-Woogie* to give people a glimpse of the future—the future as he imagined it. The pieces of sticky tape reveal his longing and impatience for that future.

Since the painting is unfinished, it seems as though time is standing still in it—as if we are looking at both the past and the future at the same moment. And indeed, Mondrian's future has become our past.

And yet... the painting also seems to be still in the process of developing, as if it were alive. There is so much life in *Victory Boogie-Woogie* that it continues to move people even after all these years.

FURTHER RESOURCES

Reading

Blotkamp, Carel. *Mondrian: the Art of Destruction*. London: Reaktion Books, 2004.

Bois, Yve-Alain, and Angelica Zander Rudenstine. *Piet Mondrian*. Boston: Bulfinch Press, 1995.

Deicher, Susanne. *Mondrian: 1872–1944, Structures in Space*. Köln: Taschen, 2000.

Fauchereau, Serge. *Mondrian*. New York: Rizzoli, 1994.

Holtzman, Harry, and Martin S. James. *The New Art, the New Life: the Collected Writings of Piet Mondrian*. Cambridge: Da Capo Press, 1993.

Joosten, Joop and Robert P. Welsh, *Catalogue Raisonné*. New York: Harry N. Abrams, 1996.

Milner, John. *Mondrian*. London: Phaidon Press, 1992.

Van Reek, Wouter. *Coppernickel Goes Mondrian*. New York: Enchanted Lion Books, 2012. (For Younger Readers.)

Watching

"Onderzoek Victory Boogie Woogie." http://www.youtube.com/watch?v=s4lGfiVyL0Y.

Life in New York

Mondrian came from the Netherlands, but he lived and worked abroad for much of his life. He wanted to live in a big modern city, because that's where he believed the future lay. His name was originally Mondriaan with a double "a," but when he moved to Paris he removed one of the a's from his name to make it easier to pronounce: Mondrian.

During World War II, Mondrian left Europe for New York. He didn't feel safe in Europe anymore because of the war, and because of Nazi occupation he felt that he soon wouldn't be free to paint as he wanted. He was already nearly seventy years old, but he loved the idea of starting over in America, and he felt enormously lucky to be able to do so. It was thanks to Harry Holtzman, on whom the Harry in the book is based, that Mondrian was able to come to New York in 1940. Harry Holtzman was a young American painter who had visited Mondrian in his studio in Paris. In 1940, he arranged for Mondrian to come to New York. In the documentary *Mondrian in New York* by Piet Hoenderdos, Harry Holtzman remembers the day Mondrian arrived in New York. Holtzman played the newest Boogie-Woogie records for Mondrian, who was very tired from the journey. On hearing the music, Mondrian was completely revived and exclaimed: "Enormous! Enormous!"

Mondrian found New York exhilarating. He loved new things and new experiences, and he was always looking for new sources of inspiration. In New York, he felt closer to the future than ever. The city gave him so much new energy that he made some of his most beautiful paintings there, and they were unlike anything he had painted before. He loved working alone in his studio, but he also liked going out with his new friends to clubs with live music, where he could dance to the latest boogie-woogie music. He tried to capture the rhythm of the music in his work, saying that he wanted to put "more boogie-woogie" into his art.

His work sold better in America than it had in Europe, so after a while he was able to move from his small first studio to a larger one on East 59th Street, close to Central Park. He thought that his new studio was the best he had ever had. As he always did when he moved into a new place, he painted the walls white and hung red, yellow, and blue painted pieces of cardboard all over them. He fixed these colored shapes to the walls with pins or tiny nails so that he could easily move them around, since he was always experimenting, looking for the best arrangement. He also made most of his furniture himself, including the kitchen table in the story and the orange-crate cupboards. This wasn't because he couldn't afford any furniture, but because he thought that his own creations suited his home better.

Victory Boogie-Woogie

In his last studio, Mondrain focused on just one painting. He had been working on it for over a year and wanted to finish it, because he was already thinking about a new painting. One that would be "bigger, and much better," he told a visitor. But first he had to finish *Victory Boogie-Woogie*. He worked on it every day, often deep into the night, and often with the latest boogie-woogie music playing on the record player.

Mondrian discovered something else new in America: colored tape. This tape made it easier for him to try out his ideas. To find out what a certain arrangement of colors would look like, he would stick pieces of colored tape onto his canvas. When everything was just as he wanted it, all he had to do

"Mondrian in New York." http://www.youtube.com/watch?v=jua8k1w0TMs.

"Piet Mondrian – A Journey Through Modern Art." http://www.youtube.com/watch?v=9fmiKOOvLU&feature=related.

http://www.moma.org/collection/artist.php?artist_id=4057 – Good biographical information about Piet Mondrian as well as lots of images of his works.

http://www2.fiu.edu/~andiaa/cg2/chronos.html – An engaging presentation of many of Mondrian's works, with commentary.

Looking
Places you can see Mondrian's work in the United States:
Boston, MA: Museum of Fine Arts
Cambridge, MA: Harvard Art Museums
Chicago, IL: Art Institute of Chicago
Fort Worth, TX: Kimbell Art Museum
Houston, TX: Museum of Fine Arts
New York, NY: Museum of Modern Art, The Guggenheim
Philadelphia, PA: Philadelphia Museum of Art
San Francisco, CA: San Francisco Museum of Modern Art
Washington, DC: National Gallery

The museum where Linus sees *Victory Boogie-Woogie* is the Museum of Modern Art (MoMA) in New York. In March 1945, there was an exhibition at the museum to commemorate Mondrian and his work. You can still see work by Mondrian at MoMA, including one of his most famous paintings, *Broadway Boogie-Woogie*, but *Victory Boogie-Woogie* is now at the Gemeentemuseum in The Hague, Netherlands.

ACKNOWLEDGEMENTS

My thanks go to Hans Janssen and Jet van Overeem from the Gemeentemuseum Den Haag, for their stories about Piet Mondrian; Willem Campschreur, Janet Moerdijk, Andrea Prins and Liesbeth ten Houten, for their enthusiasm and their input; Claudia Zoe Bedrick, who told me about American milk boxes and also put me in touch with Mr. Melvin Bedrick; Mr. Melvin Bedrick, a native of New York City, who in 1943 was around the same age as Linus and was kind enough to answer my questions about daily life at that time; Wouter van Reek, for our conversations at the kitchen table about "my" Mr. Orange and "his" Mr. Quickstep (in *Coppernickel Goes Mondrian*). They made the time when we were both working on a book about Piet Mondrian a very special one.